No Scarlet Ribbons

No
Scarlet
Ribbons

Susan
Terris

Farrar · Straus · Giroux
New York

Fic
TER

For Marilyn Sachs
who has given me friendship, advice,
and the perspective of her wonderful sense of humor

No Scarlet Ribbons

1

To her mother's wedding, Rachel Nolan brought her harp and a stray black cat from Rossi Park. While the cat slept under her chair, she plucked triumphantly at the harp strings. She played "Greensleeves," Bach's "Musette," and other songs appropriate for a bright October day.

Looking around her grandmother's apartment, she felt a sense of accomplishment when she gazed at the members of her newly made family. Yes, they were all there. Her mother, Ginger. Norm, her new father. Norm's son, Sandy, and Sandy's little sister, Kate.

Rachel liked what she saw. Everything was in place. The images before her eyes were as perfect as a series of semigloss photographs from one of Ginger's gallery exhibits. Printed. Matted. Neatly framed. Today Rachel felt protected. She was part of a whole family again.

Always, her eyes focused first on her mother. Beautiful, vibrant Ginger wearing a wreath of daisies in her red-brown hair. Ginger in a long, peach-colored peasant dress with her Rolleiflex hanging from a strap around her neck. She was bustling about taking pictures of everyone. Her cheeks were flushed with excitement. Rachel could feel a matching warmth in her own face.

Next to Ginger, staying very close to her—Norman Ross. Solid. Stocky. Serious and thoughtful. He was her eighth-grade English teacher, whom she had introduced to her mother only two months ago. As the Rosses had begun to spend more and more time at her house, Rachel had jokingly referred to them as "the Visitors." Now, however, Norm wouldn't be a Visitor anymore. He was going to be her father. She was happy about this marriage and proud to have had something to do with it.

Sandy's attitude toward the marriage had been somewhat less enthusiastic. When he was told the news, his response was expressed in one sentence: "Holy shit, Dad, you hardly know the woman!"

To that, Norm had replied with calm assurance, "Son, if things are right, they are right. And I know they are."

Rachel agreed wholeheartedly with these words. Even fourteen-year-old Sandy and his sister, Kate, suited her, she thought, scanning the room to locate their curly blond heads. She'd never had a brother or a sister before. Only Sandy would be in the house with them, but Kate—who lived with her mother—would still be part of the family. Family. A whole family. Rachel closed her eyes and leaned her head against the sounding board of her harp as she thought about being part of something safe and whole.

Her eyes were still closed when her grandmother spoke out from behind her left shoulder. "Look at your mother, Dumpling," Gram Adele said. "She's so happy. It's about time. It *is* about time . . ."

Time. Instead of opening her eyes, Rachel squeezed them tightly closed. Gram Adele's mention of time had filled her head with other images. Images she wanted to push from her mind. Ones she wanted to shut out, at least

4

for today. The word "time" always brought the shadows back. It made her eleven instead of thirteen. It carried her back into the hospital. It left her, small and frightened, caught in the shadows by the side of her father's bed.

Once more, she was watching him shrink up and die, drown in the liquid in his lungs. Fa, her father. Not yet forty. Fa, who said you had to have ideas, who said you had to make things happen. He had been wonderful, incredible. A kind of magician. He'd been able to make anything happen. Anything, except that one last thing. That he should be able to go on living.

"Why me?" he'd asked, as he'd suffered through the last few days. "Why me?"

How, Rachel wondered, would her father have felt about this day? About this wedding? About Rachel's hopes for Norman Ross? She had a lot of questions but no answers. At this moment all she knew for certain was that she had to pull herself back from the shadows.

"Angel? Where are you? Wake up, Angel," a voice called. Ginger's voice, coming from some place very close.

Rachel sprang to her feet and threw her arms around Ginger. It felt wonderful to be hugging her mother, even if the Rollei was caught awkwardly between them.

"Oh, Mother. Mom, Mom. Mommy!" she cried out. "I love you. I love you so much."

"We all love her," Norm said. He was standing near enough that Rachel could feel the warmth from his breath as he spoke. "And you, Rachel. We love you."

"Speak for yourself, Dad." That comment came from Sandy, who was sauntering by with a cup of ice.

Letting go of her mother, Rachel turned toward Sandy. "Hey, are you mad at me? What did I do?" she asked. "What's the matter? You want a hug, too?"

By way of an answer, Sandy took an ice cube and flipped it so expertly that it dropped inside the rounded neckline of her white gauze dress.

"Two points," he said, winking at his father.

"Good shot," Norm agreed.

As Rachel was wriggling about, tugging at her long dress so that the ice would fall through to the floor, she didn't have any trouble finding her voice. "Basketball. Always basketball," she declared with mock disgust. "Why, two hours without a basketball in your hands and you start to get withdrawal symptoms!"

Sandy laughed. So did Norm, Gram, and Ginger. They laughed again as Rachel grabbed a cube of Sandy's ice and poked it inside the waistband of his trousers.

Hearing the laughter, Kate came running up to them. "What's funny?" she begged in her slightly whiny way. "What did I miss? What's funny?"

"Rachel is," Ginger said, fingering her camera and looking down at Kate. "She's full of funny ideas—like being so sure that your daddy and I would fall in love. She has a head full of extraordinary ideas."

Extraordinary ideas. Again the shadows. "I have to have ideas," Rachel reminded herself. With the family pressed in so close, her head felt empty of all ideas. Her cheeks were warmer than ever. Burning. The apartment felt too hot, too stuffy. She found herself wishing she had her red cape and roller skates, wishing that she was gliding through Rossi Park taking a breath of fresh, cool San Francisco air.

Ideas. Fa used to be the one with ideas. Fa, not Rachel. Nothing had ever been ordinary when he was around. They hadn't just played with ice cubes. That was ordinary. Rachel needed a whole family, but she also longed for one that was exciting. Was Norm, she wondered, ever

6

going to think up exciting, spontaneous ideas? She wasn't sure. Maybe she'd have to be the one. That might be all right, though. She could already feel an idea bubbling up from deep inside her. A good one. An extraordinary one.

"I just thought of something," Rachel sang out, playing a long, rippling chord on her harp. "Let's go to the zoo. Let's go ride the old merry-go-round. Spin around on horses and tigers and ostriches. Take a magical wedding trip. All of us. Our family. Can we, Mom?"

As Rachel was speaking, Ginger began to smile so broadly that little arcs fanned out from the corners of her eyes. Turning, she looked over at Norm. "Mmm . . . well, honey?"

Norm reached out and took Ginger's hand. He was smiling, but at the same time he was shaking his head. "Quite an idea, Rachel. But not for today. Why don't you play the harp for us again? I really enjoy hearing you play. Besides, we do have some guests."

Rachel had forgotten about the few other guests who'd come to the wedding. Although she'd heard what Norm said, she wasn't ready to give up yet. "Oh, please. It would be so much fun. A special celebration. Almost unreal."

"Unreal is right," said Sandy.

"I'd like it," Kate whispered softly.

Norm gave Kate a little squeeze. "Another time, I promise, we'll ride the carousel. But not our wedding day. Maybe Rachel can write a story about it as if we'd done it. What about it, Rachel? Can we substitute fantasy for reality? Hand it to me for class, and I'll marvel at your originality."

Norm was being nice. Almost too nice, she thought. But stiff. Firm, too. There would be no riding on the merry-go-round today.

Sandy's opinions were somewhat different. "Ride a merry-go-round? Weird, Rachel. That's what I think of that idea. Some of your others, too. Like roller-skating to school. Or bringing a stray cat with you today."

Rachel backed up and eased herself into her chair. Beginning to chuckle, she tipped the harp back onto her right shoulder. She was feeling all right again. Sandy was critical, but he was noticing her. And Norm *had* appreciated her originality. He did have possibilities.

"And a black cat at that," Sandy continued.

"Bad luck? You think black cats bring bad luck?" Rachel asked, still chuckling.

Sandy's reply was another ice cube. As she felt it sliding down inside her dress, she looked up mischievously. "So show me," she said to her family, "show me where it says, 'Do you take this boy for your lawfully wedded brother?'"

2

"Show me where it says," Rachel called out as she knocked on the bathroom door, " 'Do you take this boy for your lawfully wedded brother?' " She rattled the doorknob. "Sandy!"

"What do you want?" he answered, his voice muffled and cracking slightly.

"Trick or treat for UNICEF," she told him.

"What's that supposed to mean?"

Rachel untied her red velvet cloak—her moth-eaten, three-dollar Goodwill bargain—and dropped it on the floor next to her roller skates. "Hey, Sandy, it's Halloween, remember?"

"So what? What do you really want?"

"Why is it you're always hogging the bathroom?" she replied, choosing to answer his question with a question.

"Am I?"

"Yes," Rachel answered. "Now, please let me in. I need a ribbon to tie back my hair before we carve pumpkins."

"Yeah, okay. In a minute."

Rachel leaned closer to the door. "How about a short minute? Please. My mother may have married your father, but—"

As she was speaking, the lock clicked and the bathroom door opened just wide enough that she could see Sandy's toothy, grinning face framed by its semicircle of blond hair. "How short is a short minute?" he asked. Without waiting for an answer, he shut the door and relocked it.

Rachel began knocking again. She was still at it when Norm, his arms full of underwear and socks, stepped out of her mother's bedroom at the end of the hall. Her new father. He, too, was grinning a big-toothed grin. "What's going on? If it's a bathroom you need, you can use ours."

Turning, Rachel leaned against the door as she stuffed her hands into the pockets of her ankle-length cotton skirt. "So where does it say," she asked Norm, " 'Do you take this boy?' Look, I thought having you marry Mom was a great idea, but no one—"

Before she could finish, Norm's evenly pitched voice was interrupting and answering her. "That was funny at the wedding. The first time. But, Rachel, it's beginning to wear a little thin."

Rachel wrinkled up her nose. "I guess. But Sandy never wants to join in. We haven't done any real family things."

Listening to her, Norm frowned. Then, as his lips began to form an earnest, professorial reply, he shifted his weight, nervously reaching up to scratch his face. He was just enough off balance that the stack of socks and undershorts slipped from his hands, falling to the floor in a heap. The heap was particularly colorful because of his socks. They were all red. Norm, who was color-blind, felt that if he owned nothing but red socks, he would never go out in the world with mismatched ankles.

He bent down to retrieve his things. "Maybe. But you've got to relax a little. Your mother and I were just married on Sunday. What did you think—married on

Sunday and happy ever after? Listen, let's deal with this family thing one step at a time."

Rachel didn't answer. The tone of his voice was warm enough, but she was being lectured. She did not like to be lectured. Her mother never spoke to her that way. It made her feel uncomfortable. Very young again.

"How about it, Angel?" Norm asked.

"I don't think I want you to call me that," she said softly.

"Well, why not, for heaven sakes? Your mom does."

"Yes . . . but it was my father's name for me. Because I was born on Christmas Eve, because he thought I looked angelic sitting behind the harp. Mmm . . . don't know, but when I hear you say it, it doesn't feel right."

Before Norm was able to answer, Sandy unlocked the bathroom door and opened it. Caught off-guard, Rachel fell backward, landing on her bottom, with her skirt tangled about her legs and the wheels of one of her roller skates digging into her left shoulder. She was still sprawled in that undignified position when Sandy stepped over her.

He was shorter than Rachel. There was an unmistakable athletic bounce to the way he moved. "Hi, Sis," he said mockingly. "Hi, Dad. When you're finished with your Jockey shorts, maybe we can put up the hoop and shoot a few, huh?"

"What?" Rachel asked, leaning forward and pulling down her skirt. "Basketball? I thought we were going to carve pumpkins."

"Not me," Sandy told her.

"Yes. All of us. It's a *family* activity. See what I said, Norm?"

Sandy looked over at his father and then back at Rachel. "I'm not carving pumpkins," he insisted.

"Oh, please."

Sandy glared down at her. "Oh, get lost, will you?"

"The same to you," she shot back, aware that Norm was kneeling, watching the two of them without having the foggiest idea of how to handle the situation.

As she looked at Norm digging helplessly at his pile of socks and underwear, she could feel herself beginning to get an idea. Something that involved digging. Something more original than jack-o'-lanterns. A Halloween idea for Norm and Sandy. For herself, her mom, and for Kate, too. She'd tell them in just a few minutes.

Getting up from the floor with newfound energy, she tugged at the sleeve of Sandy's shirt. "Hey, look, I'm sorry," she said. "Okay, forget about pumpkins. But your sister—she's in the kitchen waiting for me. Would you tell her I'll be right there?"

Next, Rachel stepped into the bathroom and closed the door behind her. The bathroom was filled now with African violets that belonged to Sandy. Every ledge, every windowsill and shelf held his furry leaved, pink-and-purple-flowered collection. For a moment, Rachel stood on one foot so distracted by the violets and by her Halloween idea that she was unable to remember what she'd wanted in there. "A ribbon," she recalled at last, ". . . for my hair . . ."

As she spoke, she turned toward the closet. She was reaching in for a ribbon when she realized that something alive was curled up on a stack of striped towels. It was a cat, her latest stray. After the black one from her mother's wedding day had wandered off, she'd found this one. Demi, she was calling him, because of the odd way in which his face divided up into half gray fur and half white.

Grabbing hold of a red ribbon, Rachel turned from Demi to the mirror over the sink. "Hair," she murmured, looking at hers and thinking of Ginger's rich auburn mane. Fa used to tell Rachel that she had possum hair. Cat eyes and possum hair. She remembered this as she was examining her reflection, wondering why she didn't have any of her mother's radiant beauty. A definite "medium," she decided. Medium-tall, medium-developed, and only medium-pretty. Especially because of the impossible possum hair whose wispy brown strands would never stay tied in a ribbon.

"Hair . . ." she repeated, picturing the Rosses with their wild blond heads. They weren't the Visitors anymore. In less than a week patterns were developing that made her feel uneasy. Despite the possibilities of a man whose trademark was red socks, Norm was being disappointingly dull and formal. She had something she wanted to ask him, yet she didn't think she could unless he loosened up. As for Sandy—he never seemed to think about anything except food and sports. Although Kate was a girl who shared Rachel's interest in books, she did whine. And tattle. The Rosses simply were different from Rachel, different from her mother.

While Rachel was thinking, a series of delicate, splashy noises interrupted her thoughts. She turned around. Demi now was poised on the edge of the toilet seat, lapping water out of the bowl. She was staring at him when, all of a sudden, his bony cat's body reminded her of Halloween and of her Halloween idea. She needed ideas like that so that her new family could have fun together the way she and Fa and Ginger had.

"Yes," she told herself, flinging the bathroom door open and rushing out into the hall. "Mom?" she called. "Kate, is

Mom with you, or did she go back down to the darkroom? Norm, Sandy—come to the kitchen. Please. You see, I've got this plan . . ."

Rachel could feel her cheeks beginning to flush with anticipation. She was happy when she found that Norm and Sandy were already in the kitchen drinking milk with Kate. Ginger didn't respond immediately, but after several minutes, she came rushing up from the darkroom and joined them.

Lunging forward, Rachel threw her arms around her. "Let's have a Halloween happening, Mom."

"Wonderful," Ginger declared. "I love it already. What? Where? Tell us. Can I take pictures? When?"

"Now," she answered, stepping back. She tugged at the bottom of her sweatshirt and noticed with pleasure that, as usual, she and her mother were dressed alike. They were both wearing long cotton skirts and old sweatshirts.

"Come on," Ginger urged. "Out with it."

Rachel put her hands on her hips. "Well . . . I thought maybe we could go to Bakers Beach and have a sand sculpture contest. We'll take buckets and shovels. We can sculpt bats, haunted houses, giant spiders. And we'll ask everyone on the beach to join in."

"A sand sculpture contest?" Norm asked, scratching his head. "Today? I thought we were going to get unpacked."

"I thought we were going to put up the basketball hoop," Sandy said.

Kate didn't say anything. She simply closed the book she was holding and looked at Rachel with wide-eyed wonder.

Ginger nestled next to Norm. "How can we pass up a sand sculpture contest? We didn't ride the merry-go-round on Sunday. Let's sculpt in the sand!"

"Not me," Sandy said. "I'm not going to make a fool of myself."

Norm was frowning. Looking nervous, he kept shifting his gaze from one face to another. Finally, he spoke to Ginger. "Not that Rachel's plan isn't wonderful. Still, Sandy shouldn't have to if he doesn't want to."

"It's got to be all of us," Rachel pleaded. "We're a family now." She was feeling uncertain, worried that this chance to do something together was going to slip away.

"Come on, Dad," Sandy said. "Tell her to go play on her harp. This isn't your kind of thing, either. Anyway, it's supposed to rain. Besides, it's weird, crazy, and I'm not going to do it."

"Yes . . . Oh, yes," Ginger insisted. "Let's be spontaneous."

In less than an hour, Rachel and her family were at the beach. Moaning, groaning, and muttering swear words under his breath, Sandy was tagging along behind the others.

As soon as the five of them were down near the water, Rachel flung her red cloak behind her shoulders and began scooping up mounds of wet sand to build an enormous haunted castle. "Help me, Sandy," she urged. "Come on. Or if you like, I'll show you how to fly off the dunes."

Sandy made a face. He did not want to help, nor was he curious enough to ask about flying off the dunes. Determined to prove he had come only because he'd been pressured to do so, he sat staring out at the bay, the ocean, and the Golden Gate Bridge.

Since he wouldn't join in, Rachel helped Kate get started on a jack-o'-lantern and her mother on an intricate spider web. Then she spent some time with Norm. She wanted to be sure he was enjoying himself. Although he was not looking particularly enthusiastic, he was trying to mold a sleeping cat.

Once Rachel was satisfied that they had begun, she raced up and down the beach inviting others to be part of the contest. Soon, she was pleased to see that other sand sculptures were taking shape at the water's edge. Elated, Rachel hurried back to her castle. While working on it, she was already picturing how it would be when finished. With her cape for a costume, she'd hunch herself over, cackle, and pretend to be the spooky witch that haunted it.

As she heaped up more and more sand, she kept an eye on Sandy. And on the sky. She couldn't keep rain from falling, but she might have to keep Sandy from disappearing. Norm had said he had to come along, but no one had said he had to stay.

Rachel was still mulling this problem over when she realized that her mother had given up sculpting in favor of taking pictures. She was busy clicking shots of Norm patting sand on the backside of his lumpy cat, of Kate poking her head into the crater of her jack-o'-lantern. Then, turning, Ginger snapped pictures of other people, other half-finished works of art. After a while, she began to concentrate on shots of Sandy: Sandy sitting and sulking, Sandy jumping up and preparing to stalk away.

"Wait," Rachel called out to him. Her family event was about to disintegrate. "Don't go."

"Stay, Sandy," Kate pleaded.

"Shut up," he told her. "You stay out of this."

As Sandy spoke, Kate's eyes filled with tears. "Daddy . . ."

"Don't whine for Dad, and don't cry. You're always crying."

"Leave her alone," Rachel said, leaping up so she could place herself between Sandy and Kate.

"Witch!" Sandy yelled, making sure he could be heard over the sound of the wind and the waves. "You're starting to walk all over my life. You are the Witch of the Universe!"

"Daddy," Kate protested, wiping at her eyes. "Sandy called Rachel a witch."

"Shut up," Sandy said.

"Shut up, yourself," Rachel told him. "You're lucky to have a little sister who—"

"Can it, Rachel. I'm fed up with you both."

Distressed, Rachel looked over at Norm. She'd never been part of a sister-brother argument before. "Talk to Sandy, please. Make things better. Say something."

Norm didn't say anything.

Rachel threw her arms up in the air. "Mom, Mom! Are they still the Visitors? And always going to be the Visitors?"

"Stop them, Norm," Ginger begged. "We were having a terrific day, and all of a sudden they're bickering."

Norm didn't budge from where he was kneeling, nor did he seem capable of making any effort to help.

"Sandy called Rachel a witch," Kate repeated, enunciating clearly.

"The Witch of the Universe," Norm said, looking almost removed from the emotions swirling around him. "That's quite a phrase. It has flair."

Rachel was feeling more and more upset. Norm had retreated into his English-teacher role. Her mother was talking to him as though the others weren't there.

"Mom!" Rachel pleaded. "Norm!"

"I'm leaving," Sandy announced abruptly. "I'm going to

the gym to shoot free throws, and I may not come back for a week."

Thoroughly discouraged now, Rachel searched desperately for some way to patch things up. Her family outing seemed doomed to failure. Then she realized she had to create a new diversion. So gripping the frayed edges of her cape, she began to move as fast as her long skirt would allow. She ran straight for the dunes and started scrambling up them. Ignoring the cold drops of rain that were beginning to pelt down on her head, she pulled herself all the way to the top. She was thinking of Fa now. About to do something he might have done.

Taking a deep breath and a giant leap into space, Rachel flung herself off the dune, letting the velvet cape whip out behind her. Somehow, she knew they were all watching her—Norm, Ginger, Kate, Sandy.

For one, long, beautiful instant her arched body was poised in midair, suspended by an updraft of ocean wind. A moment later, with a thud that caused a stabbing pain in her right ankle, she landed. She didn't care about falling, though, or about her ankle. She'd been airborne, she knew, at least long enough to attract their attention. Perhaps if they began by paying attention to her, she could win their love. Help them change. Still have the chance to be part of a whole happy family.

3

"Well, Sandy did go to the beach with us last week, Rachel," Norm said, as he turned off the ignition of the VW van. "So you might reconsider about coming to his basketball game this afternoon."

Rachel sighed. "But that's such a waste of time."

"Sandy thought the beach was a waste of time . . ."

"Except when I flew. That impressed him, didn't it?"

Norm laughed, but then his face became serious again. "If we are going to be a family," he said, rattling the keys nervously, "everyone is going to have to give a little. Look, I gave up *my* Datsun, and we kept your mom's old van so we'd have it to move *your* harp."

As he was talking, Rachel was already opening the door and jumping down to the sidewalk in front of her house. When Norm said "family," it sounded stuffy, and yet that was what she wanted. Nodding, she looked back at him. "Maybe I will go," she said. "But first we should unload the harp. Sitting around outside is bad for the strings."

Rachel went back to clamp the wheels on it. Then, with Norm doing most of the work, the two of them eased the six-foot-tall, eighty-pound instrument out of the van, along the sidewalk, and into the house. As soon as the harp had been wheeled to its place in the dining room, Norm went to the darkroom to find Ginger. Lingering, Rachel thought about the carols she'd be playing in the Jefferson Christmas concert. As she was removing the harp pad and wheels, Demi appeared, stretching out of an afternoon sleep, flicking his tail against her ankles. Smiling down at the cat, Rachel plucked a few tentative chords. Then she seated herself, tipped the harp back on her shoulder, and played the same series of chords over a second time and a third.

In their house, the harp had wonderful tones because neither the living room nor the dining room had any furniture in them. After buying the house, her parents had only gotten as far as covering the floor with a fluffy white Greek carpet. Then her father had gotten sick. Now, except for the harp and a few floor cushions, the rooms were still empty, leaving a large satisfying cavern to echo back as she played.

Dreamily, Rachel began to play "Scarlet Ribbons." After that she launched into the one-minute "Solfegietto," shivering as its sad-sweet sounds floated around her. Next, she began on Bach's "Preludium," losing herself until she was conscious of little except fingers plucking, feet on pedals, as the music filled all the empty spaces inside her body and made her feel warm.

Playing on, she was only vaguely aware that Sandy was lounging in the kitchen doorway staring at her. Finally, his presence became so distracting that she stopped. "What are you looking at?"

"You," he answered, stuffing chocolate cookies into his mouth as he spoke. "When you play, you look like you're somewhere else. Outer space, maybe."

"That she does," another voice chimed in. It was Norm, who had appeared with her mother. "Sounds good, too."

"Glad *you* like it," Sandy said. "I think it's strange."

Then, flashing a smudgy, brown-toothed grin in her direction, he turned and headed off toward the gym.

Rachel looked at Norm. "He's not very adventurous. I think, if I try harder, I could probably have a good influence on him."

"Did it ever occur to you," Norm asked, "that he might not want to be changed?"

Before Rachel had to answer, her mother spoke. "Hi, Angel. How was school? Did the harp sound wonderful with the orchestra?"

Norm and her mother were standing very close together, as they always did. It had never bothered her before. Suddenly, though, it made her feel left out. Made her want to phone Gram Adele and see if she could go over to her apartment for a visit. Or stay overnight.

She fastened her eyes on Norm. Being left out was upsetting. "Hey, Norm . . ." she said, speaking tentatively.

"Yes?"

"When do we leave for the game?"

Ginger gazed up into Norm's face. "What game? Who's going to a game?"

Feeling a comfortable warmness return to her cheeks, Rachel put the harp back in place, bent down, and pulled something out of her bookbag. "I am. And Norm is."

Ginger laughed. "Rachel, is this some kind of joke? You have about as much interest in sports as I do. Norm, aren't you suspicious of this girl of mine if she says she's going to a sporting event? This girl reads books and plays the harp, but she does *not* attend sporting events."

"Do you want me at home?" Rachel asked her mother. "You want me to shop or fix dinner so you can keep working in the darkroom?"

"Mmm. No, Angel. Not really, not if you . . ."

As Rachel listened to her mother's voice trail off, she

pulled her cloak around her shoulders. Next she grabbed her skates and raised her chin in the air. "Well, if you don't need me, Mom, I'll see you later. Listen, don't hold me up, please—because I'm about to have an enlightening educational experience."

Norm laughed at her comment. She hoped he'd still be amused when he found she'd put *Pride and Prejudice* under her cloak. As soon as she was seated in the gym, she was planning to pull it out, making sure that her afternoon would prove to be enlightening and educational.

"Let's cut through Rossi," Norm suggested as she was putting on her skates.

Rachel agreed. She liked having an excuse to skate in Rossi Park. In fact, she patrolled it frequently looking for signs of stray animals that might need her help. With this in mind, she glided in front of Norm, crisscrossing the path and turning her head from side to side.

As she went along, she found that she was thinking about Norm. She had a serious question to ask him. But she was afraid.

"What are you doing?" Norm called out after a while.

"Looking for strays."

"Just what we need. We already have this week's stray. Isn't that sufficient for a while?"

Pausing, Rachel shook her head. "No, never. Not if I see some animal that really needs help. Another cat . . . or a dog, maybe . . ."

"I had a dog once . . ." Norm started to tell her, but the rest of his sentence was lost as she pushed off and skated ahead again.

She didn't see any needy animals, so she tried looking for something else. Skidding to a stop, she peered into the middle of a large clump of bushes.

"Now what are you doing?" Norm asked.

She waited until he caught up with her. Then, nodding, she whispered. "Looking . . ."

"For dogs?"

"No . . . for people. Michele—you know Michele O'Leary from school—she says some people hide out in the bushes in the park. But I don't see anyone."

Stray people. Stray animals. The fact that they didn't belong anywhere frightened and fascinated her. Could Norm understand this? She wasn't sure.

"Cut it out, Rachel," he said, speaking to her in a voice that was gentle but firm. "At your age, you should have enough sense to stay away from the bushes in a city park."

Rachel started skating again, but backward this time, still eyeing the glossy green bushes edging the path. "Think how a person must feel to hide in the bushes."

"Rachel, are we going to Sandy's game? We are, aren't we?"

Her answer was not related to his question. "I hate this time of year," she mused. "It rains too much and my birthday is coming. And, of course, Fa died. Cancer is awful . . ."

Norm nodded. "I know," he told her, speaking softly.

Rachel could feel herself getting choked up. She wouldn't cry, though. She never cried. "You know? How do you know? I loved Fa, even if he did yell sometimes. Besides, you didn't watch him shrink and die."

"Please, don't get worked up," Norm begged, catching her elbow and forcing her to stop. "I'm better with rational discussions than emotional ones."

Shaking herself loose from his grip, she glided on, aware that Jefferson was now only half a block away. "When you were married to Kate and Sandy's mother—to Eleanor—you had a perfect wife and kids all together. You had a perfect family."

"If Eleanor were so perfect—or if I were—I'd still be married to her."

"I like you," Rachel murmured, ignoring Norm's words and continuing with her own shadowy thoughts. "And you look healthy, but Fa looked healthy, too, until . . . And Mom—isn't she beautiful? Beautiful and healthy. I love her, but I'm not sure I love you, even if I do *like* you. I thought we'd be closer after the wedding. But we're not."

"Your moods are so changeable," Norm complained. "First you agree to see Sandy's game, then you're hunting for strays, and now you're talking about death. Is that what's really bothering you?"

Rachel stopped and, standing on one foot, gazed back at the park. The shadows were pressing in all around her. There was a huge lump in her throat now. She had trouble finding her voice, difficulty forcing herself to ask the question. "Yes, well. Look, Norm. I can't help wondering. I mean, I get scared . . ."

"Go on," Norm urged.

"Look . . . if something happens to Mom, Norm—if she dies, do I belong to you?"

She'd said it. Now she was hoping he'd surprise her. She wanted him to answer by doing something totally out of character. By lifting her off the ground and swinging her through the air saying, "Yes! Yes! Yes!"

But he didn't. He flunked the test. All he said was "What?"

If something happens to Mom, Norm—if she dies, do I belong to you?

Rachel felt miserable. She was sorry that she'd raised the subject. She wished she hadn't asked. Turning away, she began coasting forward, gliding right up to the doorway of the gym.

"Rachel! Wait. This discussion isn't over. It's just beginning, and it's much more important than any basketball game."

"It's over," she insisted, beginning to pull off her skates.
"I can't talk about it anymore now. I just can't."

Norm looked very concerned. "Listen, Rachel. We
should talk. What's wrong with now?"

"Maybe some other time. But not now. If you try and
make me talk now, I'll go home. Really I will." At that
moment, she would have been very happy to find herself
skating home to her mother.

"Don't go," Norm pleaded.

"Then let's not talk. But let's go in," she urged. "I want
to find Sandy. Where is he?"

Reluctantly, Norm followed her into the gym.

"Where is he? I can't find him," Rachel said, as she
looked down at ten boys chasing each other around the
gym floor in outfits that appeared to be colorful sets of
matching underwear.

Norm pointed. "There—where he usually is. Where
most of the short boys are. On the bench."

To keep the sweat smell from prickling inside her nos-
trils, Rachel was trying to breathe shallowly. "On the
bench! You mean he wastes all this time, practices every
day, to sit on the *bench*? So that's why he spends so much
time in the bathroom. He's busy picking all the splinters
out of his bottom!"

She had hardly finished locating Sandy, and making
this joke at his expense, when she noticed someone familiar seated in the wooden bleachers. Her mother was
watching the game through the lens of a camera, snapping
one picture after another. Ginger must have driven the
van to Jefferson to have the fun of surprising them.

Finding her there made Rachel feel relieved. Now she

25

and Norm would not have to have any dangerous discussion. The three of them would watch Sandy's game. Then, afterward, she began telling herself, the four of them might do something wonderful. Like buying Russian piroshki and Chinese dim sum snacks on Clement Street and having a sunset picnic on Twin Peaks.

To make the time before the picnic pass quickly, Rachel started cracking jokes about Sandy on the bench, but her mother didn't laugh. Instead, Ginger put her camera aside and began asking Norm earnest questions about basketball strategy. Rachel stopped joking. She felt invisible. Though she considered pulling out her book, she didn't. She just sat there watching the harshly lit gymnasium floor as visions of piroshki, dim sum, and a panoramic sunset faded slowly away.

Silently, she waited for the game to end. At last, when Sandy's team had gone down to a dreadful 57 to 28 defeat, Norm stood up. He looked at Rachel and her mother. "Ready to go?"

Rachel didn't move. "Not me. I'm going to wait for Sandy."

Standing up, Ginger tugged at Rachel's cloak. "Come on, honey. Staying will only embarrass Sandy. Is that what you're trying to do?"

Embarrassing Sandy was not what she had in mind, but even that would be better than tagging along with Norm and Ginger when they were ignoring her and discussing sports. She was feeling hurt. At the moment, she thought she'd rather concentrate her energy on Sandy. She could work on making friends with him while she was figuring out how she was going to handle the way she was feeling about Norm, the way she was feeling about Norm and Ginger together.

Despite her mother's objections, Rachel wouldn't budge. She stayed while they left. After she'd put her skates back on, she leaned against the wall opposite the locker room reading *Pride and Prejudice*. When Sandy finally appeared, he walked right by without noticing her because he was deep in conversation with two boys, one tall and one short.

"Sandy," she called, gliding after him, "wait up."

At the sound of her voice, he came to an abrupt halt. "Oh, no," he groaned.

"Who are you?" the tall boy asked.

Rachel gave him a pixie-like grin. "Sometimes Sandy calls me the Witch of the Universe. Of course, he doesn't really mean *witch*. He means one that rhymes with it and starts with a 'b.' But he won't call me that in front of his father."

As she said this, Sandy's friends began to laugh. She had hoped Sandy would be amused, too. But he wasn't. He was furious. "Rachel! Shut up. Look, you guys, cut it out. She's just my sister."

"He's lying," the short boy called out. "Sandy's sister is that shy little midget with the electric yellow curls."

Disgusted, Sandy signaled for them to be quiet. "This is Rachel Nolan—my *stepsister*. Remember when I couldn't go to the Marx Brothers' festival because Dad was getting married and I was moving? Well, this is the reason."

"Sometimes I think Sandy hates me," Rachel told the other boys. "He says I'm stepping all over his life."

"Well, you are. But I don't hate you," Sandy replied with elaborate politeness.

"You don't? Good." She meant it, too. She wanted Sandy to like her. If he didn't, she'd never be able to improve him, never manage to create the kind of family she had in mind.

The tall boy shook Sandy by the shoulders. "Come on, be nice. Tell us more about your *sister* here."

Sandy grinned in a way Rachel recognized as being slightly malicious. "She skates. She wears funny clothes. And . . . she reads books."

"Doesn't everyone read books?" Rachel asked, deciding it was time to take charge of this conversation. "Well, maybe Sandy doesn't." Sandy's friends' grins encouraged her to continue. "Poor Sandy, he's having a terrible time with his family. He's got an English teacher for a father, a supersensitive little sister, and now he has the rest of us. My mother who takes pictures all the time. And me. He even has to put up with my grandmother, who lives nearby. She keeps a knitting needle in her hair and lives with a dummy."

"A dummy?" the boys asked.

Smiling, Rachel blew a stray lock of hair out of her face. "Yes, his name is Walter. He's a blow-up dummy who sits in her car and rides with her to nighttime bridge games. She thinks Walter protects her from muggers. And the knitting needle—that's for protection, too."

"Shut up, Rachel," Sandy said.

Rachel was feeling good. Except for Michele, she didn't have many friends these days. Since Fa had died, she'd been too busy with Ginger, too busy thinking. But Sandy's friends seemed to appreciate her. She liked that. Maybe she could make them into her friends, too.

"What am I going to do?" she asked them, turning in a circle on her skates. "He tells me to shut up. I told you he hates me."

"I'm beginning to," Sandy growled, looking as if he might butt his head into her stomach and send her flying through the air.

"Cut it out, Sandy," the short boy insisted. "We like

your sister. Even if she does read books and dress funny. But tell us—what *else* does she do?"

This time Sandy's grin was not just somewhat malicious but positively evil. "She plays a harp."

"A harp?"

"Come on, you're kidding."

"No, really. I swear. She plays a weirdo harp!"

Rachel was about to say something fiery in defense of harp playing when the tall boy spoke up again. "Listen, Ross," he said, taking a good look at the front of Rachel's sweatshirt, "don't complain. Even if she is unusual. Not every guy we know gets to have his own live-in girl!"

Rachel laughed along with the others. She could feel her cheeks glowing with a combination of pleasure and embarrassment.

4

"I'm doing everything I can to make friends with Sandy, but he still hates me," Rachel said at the dinner table that night.

Sandy was ignoring her, because he was angry about the scene she'd staged with his friends. By bringing up the subject in front of her mother and Norm, she hoped to have a discussion that would ease some of the tension between them.

Rachel leaned her elbows on the table. "Can I get anyone more salad? More spaghetti? Sandy? Sandy, talk to me. Why do you hate me?"

"I don't," he mumbled, swiping at a dangling strand of spaghetti. "How many times do I have to tell you that?"

"Well, if you don't hate me, you don't *like* me."

"Leave me alone. Shut up," he told her between gulps of milk.

Norm frowned. "Hey, you two. What's going on? How did this get started?"

Leaning forward, Ginger spoke up. "I know. The same way things often get started when Rachel's around. She acts innocent and says something inflammatory. Okay, Angel, what went on after the ball game today? What happened?"

"Nothing," Rachel said.

"Nothing? Well, maybe that's what's bothering you. I think you're pushing too hard."

Norm scratched the side of his face. "What did she say? Just asked Sandy why he wasn't making more of an effort, which may be a reasonable question."

Rachel was beginning to feel angry. Her mother and Sandy got along well. Almost too well. Instead of criticizing Sandy and supporting her, Ginger was doing just the opposite. "Mom's not being fair," she grumbled.

"I agree with you, Rachel," Norm said. "And, Sandy, I think you ought . . ."

As Norm was speaking, Sandy drained the last of the milk from his glass. "I'm leaving," he said. Then, pushing back his chair, he stood up and fled from the room.

"Me, too," Rachel chimed in. Jumping up, she pursued Sandy down the hall and upstairs. But he was quicker than she was. By the time she reached the top of the stairs, she could already hear the bathroom door slamming and the lock being clicked into place.

"Sandy!" she called. "Sandy!" As she was calling, she was already banging.

After a long silence, he answered. "Rachel?" his voice was surprisingly close, right on the other side of the door.

"What?"

"Nothing. I just wanted to know if you were still there."

"Of course I'm still here."

"What do you want?"

Rachel stepped forward so that her mouth was right next to the crack in the door. "Why can't we be friends?"

"I don't know," he said, sounding as if he was leaning his face against the door frame.

"Oh, come on. You must know."

"Well, I don't," he insisted. "Why do you spend so much

time watching me, working me over? I'm not such a terrible person. I play ball and do a little theater stuff at school. I grow African violets. You make me squirm. And you make my dad nervous, too."

What Sandy was saying made her feel uncomfortable. "Me?"

"Yes, silly," he hissed. "I told Dad it was too soon to get married. 'Angel,' your mother calls you. Don't you think that's kind of an ironic name for *you?*"

"Ironic. Why, Sandy, what big words you use."

"Shut up. You're so sure of yourself. So bossy."

Feeling sorry that she had let her tongue get the best of her, Rachel tapped her fingers lightly against the closed door. "I don't mean to seem that way," she told him, speaking truthfully. "I don't have many friends. No one I can really count on, except my mother. Michele O'Leary —she's kind of half a friend. And, you know, since Fa died, I'm sort of half an orphan."

"Half an orphan!" Sandy exclaimed. "You feel sorry for yourself, so we're supposed to feel sorry for you?"

"No—okay, take that part back. But my father did die. And I do feel—I don't know—scared a lot of the time. Don't you ever feel scared, Sandy?"

"Me?" he said, but his voice was faint. This conversation, Rachel realized suddenly, was getting too personal for him.

She changed the subject. "Sandy, can't we be friends? The kind of friends who do things together?"

His answer was silence.

"Sandy, can't we be friends?"

"Probably not. Especially since you're always making me do things I don't want to do. When does my turn come? When do I get to make you do something?"

32

"Any time," she answered agreeably. "Tomorrow? The day after?"

Sandy groaned. "Next year, maybe."

"What about sooner?" she asked softly.

There was another long silence, but she could still hear him breathing only a few inches away. "Well, I'll think about it," he said, at last. "Now go away, will you? Just leave me alone."

"Yes . . . in a minute," she said, not wanting to let go of the conversation, stalling while she tried to think of something that might interest him. "Sandy?"

"What?"

"Listen, Michele says that sometimes people hide in the bushes in Rossi Park. You know how I look for stray animals there? Well, these are stray people. They probably need help, and we . . ."

". . . could help them? Rachel! People in bushes? What's wrong with you?"

Seeing that that subject was never going to work, Rachel dropped it immediately. "Well, then," she said, ready with another suggestion, "what about doing something together? I'd get Michele. You'd get your basketball friends. We could go roller-skating."

"Roller-skating?"

"It wouldn't have to be with our friends. I mean, we could go with Mom and Norm and Kate."

"No!" Sandy yelled through the door. "I said *I* wanted to plan something, but you—you're already doing it again. And, whatever, I am *not* going roller-skating!"

Because Sandy had been so angry, Rachel decided that she'd better ease up. So, for the next ten days, she tried hard to be more agreeable. She asked Sandy to tell her how he kept his African violets blooming so beautifully, but she didn't mention roller-skating. She went to the Conservatory for her Tuesday lessons with Madame Marzini. She practiced faithfully on the harp, making sure to thank Norm profusely each time he helped her move it to school and back. She helped her mother in the darkroom, and one Saturday afternoon she even took Kate to the movies.

But she didn't feel particularly happy. Even though they lived in the same house, they all did separate things. Finally, as Thanksgiving approached, Rachel couldn't stand it any longer. She had an idea. A spectacular way for them to spend Thanksgiving morning. Yet when she suggested it to Sandy, he exploded.

All he could manage to say to her was "No! No! No! No! And I mean *never!*"

The vehemence of his response sent her right down to the darkroom to have a talk with her mother. "Sandy should be more considerate," she said, squinting to see Ginger through the dim red developing light.

Ginger tapped Rachel on one shoulder with a pair of her long wooden tongs. "What have you got planned that he doesn't know about, but he's worrying you *might* have planned and want him to take part in?"

"I went to his basketball game," Rachel replied.

"That isn't what I asked. I knew it had been too quiet around here. The quiet before the storm. What's going on? Pushing for more togetherness?"

Twisting her fingers together in her lap, Rachel sat on the darkroom stool. Thinking, she eyed the deft way in which her mother used the tongs to transfer several more pieces of wet paper, gently pressing down on each one so that it would be immersed in solution.

"I could be good at photographing and developing, too,

if you'd ever give me the chance," she said, still eyeing her mother.

"You do have something planned, don't you?"

Rachel pushed aside the beaded light cord, which was dangling down, giving her cheek an icy tickle. "Yes, but I want Sandy to come along. And you and Norm and Kate. All of us."

Picking up an extra set of tongs, she reached out and began splashing solution over some blank papers her mother had just slipped into the developing pan. On top, a picture was coming into focus. She could see the sounding board of her harp and a rounded figure in white behind it. Herself, laughing, with the harp tilted against her right shoulder. Fa used to love to see her that way. He said it kept her in one place for more than five minutes. His angel. Rachel sighed.

"What chords was I playing?" she asked, reexamining the photograph, which showed her fingers a blur as they'd been plucking a rapid series of chords. "Ones from 'Scarlet Ribbons'?"

Looking preoccupied, Ginger moved several prints from the washing pan onto the drying rack. "I shouldn't be fussing with the wedding pictures. I have portraits of the Maier girls to do. But the money-making stuff is never as much fun. Oh, that reminds me—Imprint Gallery called this morning. They want me to be part of a group show planned for January!"

"Wonderful," Rachel said, putting down the tongs and beginning to fool with the light cord. She was interested in her mother's news but fascinated by a new piece of paper floating in the developer.

"Sandy snapped it," Ginger said, as she noticed Rachel staring.

Rachel, still twisting the light cord, kept her eyes on

35

that paper. The first thing to appear was Ginger's dark hair. Then came the faint outline of another head. Norm, turned sideways. Ginger, crowned by daisies, was facing directly into the camera, smiling, but with her eyes nearly closed as Norm was bumping against her gently. Bumping her hip and shoulder. It hadn't bothered Rachel then, but it did now.

Suddenly light flooded the darkroom.

"Rachel!" Ginger yelled. "The cord!"

The instant she heard her mother's voice, she jerked at the cord again, plunging them back into red darkness. "Oh, no, Mom! I'm sorry. Really sorry, I . . ."

Her mother wasn't listening. "You've ruined it. It's all fogged. Oh, Rachel, it took me ages with the enlarger to get it just right. Tell me you didn't do that on purpose."

"Of course I didn't," Rachel said, jumping to her feet. "I was just fooling with the cord and I guess . . . well, I must have pulled on it. I just wanted to see if we could go roller-skating on Thanksgiving. Roller-skating across the Golden Gate Bridge."

"What?" Ginger asked, forgetting how angry she'd been and looking thoroughly intrigued. This was, after all, the kind of idea Fa used to think up for them to do. Like spending an hour riding the giant hobby horses outside the Nut Tree Restaurant—all of them together.

"Roller-skating across the Golden Gate," Rachel repeated softly. "And it won't be any fun if Sandy won't come, too. But, Mom, I am sorry—so sorry—about your picture! I love your pictures. I don't want to ruin any of them. Ever."

As she was speaking, she was giving her mother a warm, apologetic bear hug. Then she turned toward the door. Pausing, she took one more look at the photo still shimmering in the pan. It was mostly white paper, with the faint outlines of two heads, two pairs of eyes, two pairs of lips.

"I like it this way," she said. "Foggy and beautiful. Not just a wedding picture, but something you could exhibit."

Ginger moved up right behind her. "Mmm . . . you're right. You solarized it by pulling the chain. And it is sensational! You do have an eye. And a wild imagination. Now what were you suggesting? That we roller-skate across the Golden Gate Bridge?"

5

"Whoever said coming out to skate across this bridge was a good idea was wrong," Sandy complained, bending down to refasten the borrowed metal skates on his sneakers. "This must be the twenty-seventh time I've had to fix these stupid things."

"It was Rachel's idea," Kate said as she zigzagged neatly past him.

"Of course it was Rachel's idea," he answered, raising his voice so it could be heard above the traffic sounds on the roadway next to the sidewalk where they were standing. "Every dumb thing I get myself into these days is Rachel's doing!"

Pretending not to hear him, Rachel leaned against the bridge's cold, orange-painted railing and looked out over the bay. Standing there on her skates, she gazed at the city of San Francisco, at Angel Island, and at Alcatraz, with its crumbling old prison buildings.

Sandy went right on grumbling. "She has her own skates and they tie on. So do you, Kate. Ginger and Dad have rented tie-ons. And I'm the only sucker here with these Mickey Mouse clamps!"

"Glorious!" Rachel declared, still staring out. "Sandy,

can't you see how beautiful everything is this morning?"

At that moment, he couldn't. Rachel was comforted, though, by the fact that Norm and Kate and her mother seemed pleased with her Thanksgiving idea.

Ginger had been so enthusiastic about the event, she'd even decided to leave her cameras at home, saying all she wanted to do was enjoy skating with Rachel and the others. They had hardly arrived at the south parking lot of the bridge, however, hardly climbed out of the van and put on their skates, when Ginger tripped over the hem of her long skirt and fell to her knees.

"Oh, no," she'd told them, laughing. "You kids better go on ahead. It's going to take us longer. Norm and I will be slow for a while."

"I'll stay and help, Mom," Rachel had volunteered. "We want to skate *with* you and Norm. We'll wait and go slowly."

"No, no," her mother'd said, pulling herself to her feet and clinging unsteadily to Norm's arm. "We'll catch up and skate with you later."

"Right," Norm had insisted, as he struggled to keep his own balance, looking as if he was beginning to wonder how he had ever agreed to cross the bridge on skates. "This is going to be quite an experience. But let us manage it at our own pace. Okay?"

Finally, Rachel had agreed to leave them behind. Skating rhythmically on the bridge, she had decided, was—for the moment—more important than togetherness. So, with a wave, she and the other two had pushed off, heading toward its towering orange peaks.

For a while, Rachel and Kate had glided along together, leaving a disgruntled Sandy clomping awkwardly a short distance behind them. Then Rachel had moved forward in smooth, even strokes, leaving Kate to supervise

Sandy's skating. To clear her head, she began humming through the chords of *"Automne."* It was her newest piece, one by Grandjany, and one that moved so fast it was impossible to play without memorizing the score.

She was still occupied this way when Kate came racing up from behind her. "Rachel! Come quick. Sandy's quitting. He says he's going home, Rachel!"

Rachel responded to Kate's words by backtracking until she found Sandy again. He was bending down, muttering his whole repertoire of swear words, and unstrapping both his skates.

"Don't quit," Rachel begged him, dropping down to her knees. "Here—let me see what I can do. Give me your key. This could be so much fun, Sandy. Don't spoil it, please."

"You may be having fun, but I'm not. And how can you skate in that freaky getup? You and your mom both. And me—even without a skirt to trip over, I'm going to break an ankle or something."

"No, you won't."

"I will. Besides, I don't want to hurt myself and spend the whole basketball season sitting on the bench."

Rachel examined his face, trying to decide if he was joking when he talked about sitting on the bench. He was, she decided, and that was a good sign, because it probably meant she could persuade him not to quit.

"Look, if I tighten it right," Rachel told Sandy in her most encouraging voice, "it won't come loose. Kate—you go on, will you? And we'll be there in a minute."

As she was talking, she was using Sandy's skate key to tighten the front clamps. She was using all the strength in her fingers, which was quite a lot, since playing a harp developed very strong ones.

"Stop!" Sandy started to yell. "You're amputating my little toes."

"Crybaby," she scoffed. Then, giving the left skate one more firm twist, she removed the key and pushed it back into the pocket of his jacket. "You'll live. And if the operation was a success, your skates won't come loose again. Now—let's go."

Without giving him time to protest, she pulled him to his feet and began to describe some of the fine points of roller-skating. "Side to side, like a duck waddles. Not straight ahead like on ice skates. Side to side. Right, now bend your knees more and glide . . ."

Because Sandy was a natural athlete, it didn't take him long to remember how, especially once he decided to try instead of complain. At that point, skating the Golden Gate Bridge became a challenge to him.

Seeing the change in his attitude, Rachel began to feel wonderful. A snapping cold breeze was blowing in from the ocean, stinging their cheeks and making their eyes water, but at least the sun was shining and the wind was blowing away all traces of city smog.

Because of the holiday traffic congestion, the cars on the bridge were going so slowly that their passengers had time to roll down windows and shout encouragement to them. Some just honked and waved, but others tried to carry on conversations as they went by. The people on the walkway were also full of smiles and comments. Rachel loved this attention, and she could tell Sandy did, too, when he finally started waving back and clowning. They were both going from side to side in long, even strokes, bumping elbows occasionally. Rachel was holding her shoulders very straight and her chin high.

"Why is your head up like that?" Sandy asked, after he had sneaked a glance in her direction.

"Don't want to spill any of it."

"Any of what?" he asked, perplexed.

Rachel jutted her chin out even higher. "Any of the way I feel."

"What's that supposed to mean? Sometimes you are weird. Truly weird."

"So what?" she answered, waving toward a station wagon whose occupants were honking at them.

"Freak," Sandy muttered. "And me, I'm going to be one, too. By the end of the day, when they take a can opener and cut me out of these skates, I'll only have seven and a half toes left."

As Sandy was talking, the two of them came rolling around the edge of one of the bridge's huge towers and almost stumbled over Kate, who was lying on the sidewalk, flat on her back, looking up.

"What's going on?" Sandy asked.

"You've got to come down if you want to know," Kate answered smugly.

"Oh, cut it out. It's the old butter-on-the-ceiling trick, isn't it, Kate?" he asked suspiciously. "You fell. Now you want us to fall."

"Rachel!" Kate pleaded, her eyes beginning to brim with tears. "Sandy's being mean again."

"Ignore him," Rachel advised.

Kate swiped at her eyes with the back of one fist. "Aren't *you* going to lie down, Rachel? Aren't you?"

Rachel didn't need any convincing. "Of course," she said. She began tugging at Sandy's arm. "Let's! Let's see what Kate is seeing." She kept pleading and pulling at Sandy until, finally, he agreed to lie down on the sidewalk, too.

Stretching herself out, Rachel gasped. Above them loomed the burnt-orange tower of the bridge with its gigantic loops of snaky cables. Above that, little strands of white clouds were being whipped past by the brisk wind. Rachel clasped her arms tightly against her chest. The tower was so immense and the sky so intensely blue that she felt as if she'd been transported into some other world.

Sandy's reaction to the scene was expressed in a single word. "Wow!" he said.

"Wow!" echoed Rachel, relieved to find he was as impressed as she was. She felt so happy. Only having her mother and Norm catch up and join them would make things more perfect.

"Everything's moving," Kate told them, speaking as one who had been down much longer than they had.

"Then get up," Sandy said.

"No . . . maybe I'll never get up. Hey, Rachel, did you ever read any of Marilyn Sachs's books?"

"Yeah, all of them. Why?"

Kate rolled over onto her side. "Well, you remember the part in *Peter and Veronica* when they were roller-skating behind a streetcar?"

"Books!" Sandy howled. "Just look up there, and tell me how you can talk about books!"

"Do you remember?" Kate asked.

She did remember, but somehow she found that she agreed with Sandy. This was not a time for discussing books. Instead, she reached into the pocket of her sweatshirt and produced three tiny red apples. Without raising her head, she passed one to Sandy and one to Kate.

Lying flat on their backs, the three of them began munching the fruit. Rachel could feel the sticky juice from the apple dribbling out the corners of her mouth, down her chin, and around the back of her neck. It felt warm and tickly, but she let it drip.

Despite the fact that the traffic noises and the rough

43

concrete under her back kept reminding her of where she was, she seemed to be somewhere else at the same time. Above. Floating. Pedestrians passing by kept saying, "Hello, down there." Most of the time either Sandy or Kate responded by saying, "Hello, up there." But Rachel was too far away to participate. Squeezing the damp apple core between her fingers, she started to sing. In a high, sweet voice she sang one of the songs she played on her harp. A song called "Scarlet Ribbons."

"I peeked in to say good night,
And I heard my child in prayer.
'Send to me some scarlet ribbons,
Scarlet ribbons for my hair.'

All the stores were closed and shuttered.
All the streets were dark and bare.
In our town no scarlet ribbons,
Scarlet ribbons for her hair.
Through the night my heart was aching
Just before the dawn was breaking . . .

I peeked in and on her bed,
In gay profusion lying there,
Lovely ribbons, scarlet ribbons,
Scarlet ribbons for her hair.

If I live to be a hundred,
I will never know from where
Came those lovely scarlet ribbons,
Scarlet ribbons for her hair."

44

Neither Sandy nor Kate sang with her. Maybe they couldn't even hear her over the sound of the wind and the traffic. But she didn't care. Singing that song reminded her of her father; yet for a change that memory didn't make her feel sad or shadowed.

She let her head roll sideways so she was looking at Sandy. "Fa—my dad—might have done something like that for me."

"Like what?"

"Like in the song," she told him. "Filling my bed with scarlet ribbons."

"But he didn't."

Rachel pulled at a strand of her hair. "Nope."

"Well, Norm won't ever do it, either," Sandy said.

"How do you know? How can you be so sure?"

Sandy laughed. "He wouldn't know a red ribbon if he saw one. He's color-blind, remember?"

Red ribbons. Scarlet ones. The chords of the song kept ringing inside her head even as she and Sandy talked. Then suddenly something occurred to her. "I wish I had my harp here."

She wasn't trying to be funny. She just said what she was thinking. But her words broke them all up. Imagining Rachel on the Golden Gate Bridge playing her six-foot harp made the three of them start to howl with laughter.

"It does have wheels," Sandy cried between gasps of laughing. "You could have brought it. We could have roller-skated right across this bridge pushing a harp!"

Rachel's response was immediate. "Let's. Another day. Let's come back and do it."

"Super! Like something out of a Marx Brothers' movie —only better," Sandy agreed. "Because it would be us doing it instead of them."

While they were still shaking with giggles at the

thought of pushing the harp on the bridge, Norm and Ginger showed up. "Oh, look," Ginger called, coasting toward them. "Look at them. They're lying on the sidewalk!"

Ginger's face was flushed and happy-looking. "Lie down, Mom," Rachel suggested, pleased to see her mother. "Come see how wonderful this is. Now. Hurry. Lie down with us."

Ginger nodded enthusiastically. "Yes, let's. Come on, Norm—us, too. If they can lie there and look up, we can, too."

"No," said Norm. "Enough silliness, Sandy. Now get up, will you?"

"Not no—yes," Ginger said, taking hold of his arm. "Yes. Us, too. You and me."

Norm shook his head. "Ginger, enough is enough. We came. We skated and had fun, but we are not going to lie down on the sidewalk."

"Mom, Mom," Rachel pleaded, wishing Ginger would step away from Norm and move closer to her. "Come on. Please. Don't be stuffy. Don't let him make you stuffy!"

"Be sensible, love," Norm said, beginning to sound irritable.

"Don't be sensible, Mom," Rachel cried out. "Anything but sensible. Not stuffy, either."

Her father had never been sensible or stuffy. Fa wouldn't have argued. He'd have been down on the sidewalk in a minute. Norm, as she was beginning to see clearly, was not at all like Fa. "Please, Mom!"

Paying no attention to Rachel, Norm talked only to her mother. "Look, Ginger. It's time to be heading back. Sandy and Kate have to be at Eleanor's by one-thirty. We have to go."

Time. Rachel sighed. Norm's mention of time had

broken the spell. Thanks to sensible Norm their glorious experience was over. Now even she didn't want to be stretched out on the sidewalk anymore.

She sat up. "Why," she asked herself, "does Norm sound so angry with Mom? If he thinks my ideas are awful, why doesn't he just get mad at me?"

6

"Sensible Norm wouldn't approve," Rachel mused as she skated along through Rossi Park.

She was on her way to the gym to watch part of Sandy's Saturday basketball practice and a stray rabbity-colored dog had chosen to follow her, butting his head into her legs and barking insistently as she glided along.

"Look—I can't take you home. Norm would have a fit . . . and my mother, too, probably . . ."

Doing her best to slip away from the dog, she found herself thinking again about Thanksgiving Day on the Golden Gate Bridge. Trying once more to make herself forgive her stepfather for being such a stick-in-the-mud. As she worked at this, she frowned at the stray and hoped he'd abandon her. He didn't. He just came right along barking, nosing at the wheels of her roller skates and jumping up to scrape his paws against her skirt. After coasting a little farther, she stopped.

"Go away," she told the miserable-looking animal. Her words were emphatic; yet instead of trying to escape, she slumped down on the nearest bench and stared at him. The bench was cold, with chunks of green paint peeling off. As soon as she had seated herself, the dog did the same. Waving his flag-like tail, he waited there expectantly.

"Go away," Rachel told him.

He didn't. So she didn't, either. She just sat on the bench running one hand through her unwashed, wind-blown hair. Then she looked down at her velvet cloak and skirt, noticing how they were decorated with muddy four-toed dog prints.

"Won't you please go away?" she repeated.

In response to her words, the animal began barking again, punctuating the air all around with anguished yelping cries. "Look," she told him. "There's no place for you at my house now. Bringing you in would screw everything up."

The dog stopped his yelping, but he didn't budge. He continued to sit with his eyes staring directly into her own. The rapt attentiveness of his inky pupils encouraged her to keep right on talking. "Sandy's really been better. He came roller-skating with me. And my mom and Norm. Even they came along. Norm still needs a lot of improving. But, look, I'll never make things work if I do something really stupid like bringing home a *dog*."

Having said all this, Rachel considered the subject closed. She stood up, but before she could move away, the dog whined and settled his hindquarters down on the draggy hem of her skirt. With a shake of her head, she bent down and scratched his neck. She tried picking through the unkempt fur, hoping to hook one finger around his collar to find out where he belonged. But he wasn't wearing one.

"Why, you are a stray," she murmured. "A poor orphan. But I can't . . . unless . . ." As she was speaking, an idea was already swelling up inside her head. Jumping to her feet, she began digging down in her skirt pocket, trying to locate a dime.

Only a minute later, she was standing in a phone booth talking to her grandmother, while the disreputable-looking dog sat on the toes of her skates, dusting the pavement with his tail and X-raying her with his limpid, pleading eyes.

"But, Gram, listen—he'd be a companion. A watchdog. He's little, but he's got a great bark. He'd be protection for you when you go out at night, much better in an emergency than a blow-up dummy like Walter."

Gram Adele's voice crackled back with opinions quite different from Rachel's. "Dog? What do I want with a dog? Especially a barking dog. Mrs. Knabe will spend all day whacking her ceiling with a broomstick. And I'm certainly not looking for the kind of companion who'd mess the carpet and get into my knitting yarns."

"*Dog*, I said, Gram, not cat. Dogs don't bother yarn. And he won't bark a lot. I mean, he just sort of yaps. Oh, please!"

Rachel was just winding up for one more impassioned plea when the dog began to howl. The sounds rising from his throat were shrill and decidedly ill-timed.

"Rachel," Gram Adele said, raising her voice meaningfully to make sure it was audible above the dog sounds, "what is this thing you have about lost animals? Why is it you feel you have to save the whole world?"

"But, Gram . . ."

"No buts. Take the poor dog to the SPCA, and then play your harp or find something else nice to do."

"The SPCA *kills*," Rachel shouted. "After they keep an animal three days, they just—"

"Dumpling, I don't want to hear about it. Now be good and . . ."

Pulling the phone from her ear, Rachel pressed the receiver back onto its holder. She was sorry she'd called. There was nothing to be done for this dog. She'd simply have to abandon him. Reluctantly, Rachel turned away. Forbidding herself to look back, she sped on toward the gym. Then, without removing her skates, she edged sideways up the steps and into the doorway. As she paused to catch her breath, she scanned the place, straining to catch a glimpse of Sandy. He wasn't there. Not playing or sitting on the bench.

Puzzled, Rachel managed to slide into the row right behind the Jefferson bench. Then, leaning forward, she tapped one of the boys on the shoulder.

"Where's Sandy Ross?" she asked.

"Sandy?" the boy answered. "He's not here. Fell, and they took him to the hospital. Couldn't even get up from the floor."

"What hospital?" Rachel asked, grabbing the boy by the shoulder.

"Don't know. Children's, I think. Probably Children's."

Without waiting to hear any more, Rachel jumped up and began making her way out of the bleachers. She was furious with herself. She'd been wasting time in the park, worrying about some lost dog, while Sandy was hurting himself, lying helpless on the gym floor, and being sent to the hospital. If she hadn't spent so much time feeling sorry for a stray, she would have been there to help Sandy.

Moving as quickly as possible, she rushed up the aisle and out of the building. Children's Hospital was only a few blocks away. On her skates, she could get there in less than ten minutes.

At the hospital entryway, she stopped long enough to pull off her skates. Then she bounded up the steps and into the hospital. She was so impatient to get inside that she could hardly wait for the electric eye to open the automatic doors. Once she had rushed through them, she stood for a moment on the tweedy, green-carpeted floor, not sure where to turn. Finally, she stuck her skates under one arm and rushed toward a large sign marked ADMIT-TING.

"I'm looking for Sandy Ross," she told the pink-smocked woman behind the desk. "Sanford Alan Ross. He broke something at school and they brought him here, I think."

"Try the emergency room," the woman answered unhelpfully.

Rachel grabbed the woman's hand. "Oh, please," she pleaded, suddenly aware she hadn't been through the doors of Children's Hospital since the day her father had died there. "Sandy—my brother—is all alone."

Something about Rachel's flushed, earnest face must have appealed to the woman, because her attitude changed. She leaned forward and picked up her telephone. In just a few minutes, she managed to come up with his name and a room number. "Two thirty-seven," she said, giving Rachel an encouraging smile. "Elevators are to the right. Second floor. And when you get out, turn right again."

Calling her thanks over one shoulder, Rachel ran for the elevator. On the second floor, she stepped out and, as she had been instructed, turned right. She didn't have to look for Sandy's room number, because the first thing she saw when she swung around the corner was Norm. Norm and his former wife, Eleanor, were standing in the hallway, so close together that their heads were almost touching. Although Eleanor was frowning, the rest of her—as always—was perfect-looking. She was wearing some kind of violet-colored outfit. Norm was patting her on the shoulder.

For a moment, Rachel felt like backing up and disappearing before they saw her. She didn't particularly like seeing Sandy's parents whispering that way. It was obvious that their mutual concern was Sandy, but Norm was her mother's husband now. He wasn't supposed to be in a public corridor patting his ex-wife on the shoulder.

Before she could decide whether to retreat, Norm looked up. "How the devil did you get here?" he asked.

"How's Sandy?" she called, moving forward to meet them. "What happened? Did he break his leg?"

"Not that bad," Norm answered reassuringly. "Dr. Crawford said he'd jumped forward at a funny angle and sprained his Achilles tendon."

"What does that mean?"

"They'll put it in a cast."

"How can he play basketball with a cast on his leg?" Rachel asked.

"He can't," Norm replied. "He'll be out for the season, I'm afraid."

"Oh, poor Sandy," Rachel groaned. Then, remembering herself, she stood up straighter, flicked her scraggly hair back from her face, and managed to smile up at Eleanor. "Hello, Mrs. Ross. Are they putting the cast on now?"

Before Eleanor could answer, Norm did. "Not yet. In about half an hour. Right now he's groggy from the painkiller they gave him."

Rachel looked at the closed door marked 237. "Can I see him? Just run in for a minute and try to make him feel better?"

This time Eleanor spoke up quickly. "I think not. Later perhaps, but not now. And why aren't you wearing shoes, Rachel? A hospital, with all its germs, is hardly the place for going without shoes."

Turning away from Eleanor, Rachel began pleading with Norm. "Please. Just for one minute!"

With a shake of his head, Norm began patting her on the shoulder just as he had been patting Eleanor. "Not now. He's supposed to rest."

Rachel pulled away. Moving quickly, hoping that neither Norm nor Eleanor would stop her, she pushed at the door and rushed into the antiseptic-looking hospital room. A room not too different from the one her father had been in. Fa. She'd said her last goodbye to him in a room like this.

"Sandy," she whispered, shivering as she tried to push the memories away.

His circle of blond hair was resting on a pillow. His face was pale and his eyes were closed. "Sandy?"

"What?" he answered in a thick, furry-sounding voice.

"It's me—Rachel."

Opening his eyes halfway, he managed a slight grin. "What took you so long?"

Smiling, Rachel moved closer to the bed. "You won't believe this," she confessed, "but I was cutting through Rossi and there was this awful stray dog I couldn't get rid of. So when I finally got to the gym, you were already here."

Sandy rolled his eyes back and forth, not seeming to have heard what she had said. She tried not to think of Fa—of how it had been when she'd visited him. She wanted to concentrate all her attention on Sandy. His pupils were large and murky.

"Can you carry me?" he asked.

"Why?"

"Because I want to get out of here," Sandy answered, letting his voice fade out and his eyes flutter shut. Then they snapped open again. "How about down the fire escape?"

Rachel laughed. "Sure. Why not? But you've got to stand up so I can put you on my back."

"Can't," Sandy told her sleepily. "My leg hurts."

"Well, then, I can't lift you up and carry you down the fire escape, can I?"

Sandy grinned weakly. "You can move a harp. Why not me?"

"But not alone, and not three floors down fire escapes. Besides, you don't have any wheels," Rachel teased, poking him gently with one hand.

"But you do," he said. "And you can sling me over your shoulder, carry me down, and skate off into the sunset with me—like the ending of some old movie. I mean, you pretend like you're Wonder Woman, anyway . . ." He paused and swallowed with a dry, slightly choked-up sound. ". . . like you're all full of weird fiery powers . . . different from mortals like us . . ."

"You're not making any sense."

". . . yes, your face . . . sometimes. Skating, harp playing, on the dunes . . . like Wonder Woman . . . or . . . or . . ."

Rachel still wasn't sure what Sandy was talking about, whether he was alert and joking or floating along on some medicated fantasy. His mouth was moving, but the rest of his body was lethargic. ". . . or . . . hmm . . . I think I'm going to cry . . ."

"Cry? You wouldn't cry, Sandy. I never cry."

"Yeah . . . well . . . you wouldn't . . ."

She felt uncomfortable with the tone this conversation was beginning to take. She didn't want to talk about crying or think about the hospital. "At least," she said, trying to be comforting, "you didn't get hurt last week when we were skating. Basketball's a respectable way to get injured. How did you do it?"

"Playing Groucho . . . with a cigar borrowed from the coach. Playing Groucho, and I've finished my basketball career for the whole year."

Rachel stared down at the white seersucker blanket cover. "I'm sorry, Sandy. Really I am. But you'll have other things to do. I'll think up lots of things we can do together."

A faint smile curved up on Sandy's lips. "That's what I'm afraid of. Worrying about. Wonder Woman with a red cape and everything . . ."

"Sandy?"

"What?"

"Are you making fun of me?" she asked.

"No . . . never. Just terrified of your strange powers. And where did you say you were when I got hurt?"

"In Rossi Park."

Letting his eyes flap closed, Sandy laughed feebly. "With a stray dog? Don't believe it. For you . . . too simple. You were probably . . . probably . . . beating the bushes looking for weirdos . . ."

7

"Okay, Sandy. I'll leave you alone," Rachel said. "I'll go over to Jefferson and watch your team play ball. Or go to Rossi and see if I can't find that poor little dog."

"I didn't say leave me alone," Sandy yelled. "I said, what is the bottle of milk of magnesia doing on my night table?"

Smiling, Rachel looked at the murky-blue Phillips bottle. Then she picked up a ball of lint from the blanket on his bed and rolled it between her fingers. "I bought it for you so you wouldn't have to spend so much time in the bathroom. What do you *do* in there?"

"Well, I'll tell you one thing for sure, for what I do, I don't need milk of magnesia!" he answered, leaning over to grab one of his crutches. "Sometimes, you know, you sound just like my mother. What do you think *I* am—your latest *stray?*"

"Sorry," she said. "I'll stop. Well . . . goodbye."

"Rachel!"

"What?"

"Never mind," Sandy told her.

Pausing in the doorway of his room, she remembered something. "Sandy, in the hospital, you said something to me. Something about me thinking I'm Wonder Woman with weird powers. What did you mean?"

"I never said anything like that!"

"Oh, yes, you did," she insisted.

"I didn't. Never. Hey, why *don't* you go away?"

Rachel flashed him a dazzling, mischievous smile. "All right. I will."

As she spoke, she was already turning her back on Sandy and sauntering out of the room. She knew he couldn't come running after her. By the time he swung his hip-high cast over the edge of the bed, reached for the other crutch, and propped himself upright, she could be down the stairs and out the door. Although he'd been home from the hospital five days, he was still no expert at getting around. But he was practicing and improving rapidly, as he looked forward to Monday, when he would be going back to school.

Rachel had had plenty of time to try and influence him this last week, but she hadn't had much success. Her copy of *Pride and Prejudice* was still on his night table in the same strategic place she'd put it before he came home. The only indication that it had been touched was a raised circle on its cover, indicating he'd used it as a coaster for some icy glass. Most of the time Sandy—impatient about being trapped in the house—seemed thoroughly annoyed with her. He simply wasn't friendly toward her as he'd been when they were roller-skating or when she'd seen him in the hospital.

There were only two things she did that seemed to stir up any interest on his part. He would stuff himself with any home-baked cookies she produced, and he would sit down at her harp if she agreed to show him how to pluck at it.

"I'm not interested in playing," he kept telling her. "I

just want to know enough to try out for Harpo in the Jefferson vaudeville show."

"Harpo wasn't a hack," she told him over and over. "He was a good jazz harpist, even if he did insist on putting it on the wrong shoulder."

"Well, not me. I don't have to be good. Harps are for women," Sandy always said, which left her explaining that, like Nicanor Zabaleta, many of the best harpists in the world were men.

She would have been happy to teach him something about the harp if he wanted to learn, but he didn't. All he wanted was to clown around. He even kept putting the harp on the wrong shoulder because that was the way Harpo did it. "Harpo played that way because he was left-handed," she kept explaining, "but you're not."

Without listening, Sandy would just brush cookie crumbs out of the corners of his mouth, grin at her, and lower the harp back onto his left shoulder. For a few days she put up with this, but by Friday she was thoroughly disgusted. She was tired of wasting so much time for such negligible results, and she was also becoming aware of a change in Norm and Ginger that she didn't like.

The more time she devoted to Sandy, the more the two of them seemed to sneak off and enjoy doing things by themselves. Rachel's notion of a family was to have the four of them together, not two and two. Seeing her mother and Norm drawing closer to each other and further from her was making her feel jealous, left out, and angry.

When Ginger announced late Friday afternoon that she and Norm were going out for a Chinese dinner, Rachel protested. She begged and pleaded to be allowed to go along with them.

"No," Ginger said over and over. "No. Not tonight. I'd like you to stay and fix something for Sandy."

Ginger didn't give in, either. She and Norm were going to have their dinner out while Rachel and Sandy had theirs at home. Rachel even offered to work out a family fondue dinner for all of them—including Kate—where they would sprawl on the white rug in the living room with pillows, candles, and a roaring fire in the fireplace.

"Maybe tomorrow," Ginger had told her. "But not tonight. Now be good, hon, and we'll see you later, okay?"

No, it was not okay, Rachel was telling herself as she stood at the back door and watched them go. Two and two were not a family . . .

As she was mulling this over, Sandy—balancing unsteadily on his crutches—hopped up behind her. Ignoring him, she kept watching Norm and her mother as they walked down the driveway toward the van. The farther they got from the house, the less parentlike they seemed to become. They kept bumping against one another. In the dark and from a distance, they could have been a pair of teenagers—one stocky and square-shouldered, one pony-tailed and vivacious.

Rachel found she was embarrassed to be standing there watching them while Sandy was standing next to her. She turned to see if he was watching what she'd been watching. He wasn't. With elaborate interest, he was examining the way the adhesive tape had been wound around the hand-grip of his left crutch.

"Sandy?" she said.

"What?" he answered, lurching backward on the crutches, putting more distance between the two of them.

For a minute, Rachel just stood there. She'd broken the silence by saying his name, but she didn't seem to have anything to discuss. Suddenly Sandy seemed like some kind of boyfriend instead of like some kind of brother. Feeling warm, she groped to find some safe subject. Dinner. "I'm supposed to heat up some stew for you . . ."

"Don't want any," he mumbled. "I'm going upstairs. And leave me alone. And stop nagging." As soon as he'd finished speaking, he began hobbling toward the stairs.

"Sandy!" Rachel called after him. Was he feeling uncomfortable, she wondered, for the same reason she was?

She didn't want him to lock himself in the bathroom for the night. She wanted company, and she needed an idea. An original one. A glance out the kitchen door gave it to her. "Sandy . . . wait!"

"Why?"

"Let's play basketball!"

"Huh, what are you talking about? Me with a cast and a bathrobe and pajamas in the dark? And you who can't even throw a Kleenex in a wastebasket without missing?"

Rachel clapped her hands together. "Yes . . . yes, that's it exactly. No, I didn't mean outside. *Inside!* With a wastebasket. Maybe we could play with a wastebasket and . . . oranges, maybe."

For a moment, Sandy stood there, thinking it over. Then he nodded. "Sure, why not? But I'm going back to bed, so we'll have to play upstairs."

Almost before she knew it, Sandy was sitting with the blankets pulled up over his cast and pajamas, instructing her in the proper way to throw an orange into a wastebasket.

"No, no, don't bend your elbow. Snap your wrist, Nolan. Move your whole arm, will you."

Rachel tried; yet no matter what she did, Sandy was still dissatisfied with her efforts. "Here, throw me one," he ordered brusquely.

She did as she had been asked, but her throw was wide

and the orange rolled under his bed. Apologetically, Rachel tossed him another, which was straight enough that he managed to snag it. "Now, do like I do. Only since you're on your feet, put your opposite foot forward. The way you're doing it, you're all off balance."

Trying to obey his instructions, Rachel heaved another orange. This time it dropped right into the basket, but Sandy still wasn't pleased. Now he was yelling at her about her elbow again.

"But I always bend my elbow. I can't play the harp unless I do."

"Well, you're not playing any stupid harp now. And, if I'm teaching you, you're *not* going to throw like a girl. Come here."

As he had demanded, Rachel went over by the bed.

"Sit down," he told her impatiently. "But turn around so your back is facing me. Yes, like that."

When she was seated, he pressed an orange into her hand, and began to rotate her whole arm with the smooth motion he'd been trying to demonstrate. "From the shoulder."

Having Sandy behind her looking over her shoulder reminded her that he had been there earlier when Norm and Ginger walked out. "Did you feel funny seeing them?" she asked, pulling away from his grip and edging down toward the footboard on his bed.

"Seeing who?"

"Mom and your dad out by the van. I mean . . . do you ever think about them and sex?"

"Sure," he answered. "There's nothing wrong with sex, you know."

Rachel pulled the ribbon out of her hair. Then, carefully, she tied it back. "I didn't say there was."

Sandy tossed one more orange into the wastebasket.

"You probably think sex is disgusting. You probably think it's disgusting that they sleep together. And what about you? Do you fool around?"

"With what?" She knew what he meant, but she didn't feel like giving herself away. Sandy's friend had called her his live-in girl. Well—she was; yet she wasn't. She liked Sandy, but she didn't think she liked him *that* way.

He looked at her with one eyebrow raised. "Sex. Kissing. Had much experience?"

Rachel drew her knees up under her chin. She was feeling very self-conscious. He could ask all the questions he wanted, she wasn't going to answer them. Nothing was going to make her admit that she hadn't had much experience.

When she didn't say anything, he continued. "Look, there's nothing wrong with sex. Or kissing. I mean, look— we're not even related really, and if I wanted to crawl down there and kiss you, I could do it."

"But you're not going to."

"Of course not," Sandy said emphatically. "Ginger and Dad left us alone because they trust us. Well, I may be trustworthy. But you? Nobody ever knows what you're going to do next!"

"Oh, come on, Sandy."

"What do you mean?" he asked with a grin. "You're the one who brought up the subject of sex. All I'm doing is talking. I'm not going to touch you, kiss you, or do anything gross."

Rachel frowned. "Who says kissing is gross?"

Sandy's face was looking unusually washed-out under its crown of blond hair. He was, she realized, as afraid of being questioned as she was. Basketball hadn't left him enough time to find out much about girls, even if he was fourteen.

When he didn't answer, she got onto her knees and began inching closer to him. "Tell me about the girls you've been with," she teased. "The ones you've kissed and made out with. I want to hear all about it."

"It's none of your business," he told her in a slightly choked-up voice.

Rachel was feeling very bold. A sound outside the house was making her feel even bolder. It was a distinctive *put-put* sound. The sound of their VW van. Norm and her mother were not supposed to be back yet, but there they were. Rachel thought it was funny. She was pleased that they were about to appear unexpectedly and find her fussing around in Sandy's bedroom. She was going to surprise them by playing a joke. Just a harmless little joke.

Without hesitating for a minute, she began crawling up the bed toward Sandy. She moved to where he was slumped against the pillows looking stunned. Then pulling back the blanket, she put her bare feet under the covers next to his. She edged so close to him that she could feel the static electricity between her arm and his. Sandy tried to move away, but he could only shift over an inch or two without being in danger of tumbling out of the bed, cast and all.

"Oh, please, Sandy," Rachel urged, moving still closer to him and talking in a loud, animated voice. "I want to find out . . . I want to find out *everything . . .*"

As she was bumping against his shoulder and shouting the word "everything," Norm and her mother appeared in the door of the bedroom. Their hands were filled with white cartons containing take-out Chinese food.

Sandy looked like a corpse. His pale face was frozen into a strange, lopsided grin.

Rachel, smiling, looked up at the two stunned adults.

"We didn't expect you back so soon," she said. She made no move to get out from under the covers or off the bed.

"Obviously!" Ginger answered angrily. "It's quite obvious you didn't expect us."

"What's going on here?" Norm asked. "Why are . . ."

Not waiting for him to finish, Ginger interrupted. "Get out of there, Rachel, and tell me what's going on. God, why wasn't I more suspicious when you started all this buddy-buddy stuff with Sandy?"

"But, Mom . . ." Rachel protested, not moving an inch.

"Pipe down and let me finish. And—get out of that bed!" her mother ordered. "Look, we changed our minds. Brought back dinner to *share*, and this is what we find. Is this what you call family togetherness? Answer me. Both of you. Just what are you doing? What, Rachel, what?"

When Ginger finally had to pause for breath, Rachel was ready to answer. "Oh, you wouldn't understand," she said, feeling guilty yet giddy. She slid out of the bed and turned back to tuck the covers in around the panicky-looking invalid.

"Oh, I understand," Ginger answered. "I saw the two of you in bed together. I'm not blind, you know—or stupid."

Rachel, who never giggled, was standing there giggling, watching as Sandy's face began to regain some trace of its normal coloring. "Nothing was going on," he said, finding his voice. "Nothing."

"Don't tell me that."

"Ginger," Norm pleaded, "don't lose your temper. Let's discuss this rationally. Give them a chance to answer."

"Why? Ever since we've been married Rachel has been up to things, haven't you, Angel?" her mother demanded, paying no attention to Norm's quieter approach.

Although Rachel could see how desperately her mother

and Norm were looking for some kind of explanation, she couldn't swallow her fit of giggles long enough to tell them that it was all a joke. She had gotten even with them for going off without her, but now she had no idea how to bring the situation back under control. So as Ginger kept accusing, Rachel kept giggling.

Finally, though, she managed to take hold of herself. "Will you believe me if I tell you we were playing basketball?"

"Basketball?" her mother gasped incredulously.

Rachel nodded. "Basketball with oranges and a wastebasket."

Suddenly Rachel didn't feel like laughing anymore. Her mother and Norm were standing too close again, reminding her of how she'd felt as she watched them walking toward the van. What had happened to her mother's sense of humor, she began asking herself, and why did Norm stare that way? Something inside her head was sending throbbing signals down to her tongue, daring her to say something outrageous to add to the shock and upset they already felt.

Once, her mother would have laughed at finding her, fully dressed, sitting in bed with Sandy. But no more. Rachel interested in Sandy? That was a real joke, but Ginger couldn't see it. Some family. Her efforts to improve them were meaningless. Not only had Rachel *not* gained a father; she was also losing a mother.

"We were talking about sex," she said, looking right at Norm and Ginger. "Sandy and I don't think sex is disgusting, do you?"

8

"I don't think sex is disgusting, do you, Gram Adele?" Rachel asked.

"I'm not going to discuss my sex life with you," her grandmother replied, gesturing with her extra knitting needle. "But I do want to know how long you're planning to be my house guest. I was doing quite well on my own before you decided to move yourself in. Now, just how long *are* you planning to stay?"

"Don't know," Rachel answered. "It depends on Mom. I thought by now she'd be begging me to come back, but she isn't."

As Rachel was speaking, she walked up and down fingering the leaves on Gram Adele's plants. "I'd like it here with you if it weren't so quiet. You don't even talk to your plants or anything. Look, I know I'm not supposed to see Sandy, but maybe I can find a friend who wants to come over."

"No," Gram said, replacing the extra needle in her hair and making the pair in her hands click emphatically. "It's enough with you and the harp. Mrs. Knabe downstairs is already broomsticking the ceiling and complaining to the manager." Pausing for a moment, she finished a row, flipped over the rose-color sweater she was working on, and started racing back in the opposite direction. "Also, I don't want you to get too comfortable here."

"I thought I was your *guest*, but you make me feel like I'm in jail or something," Rachel complained, distressed to find that a whole stem of wandering Jew, fragile and pale with oblong stripy leaves, had suddenly snapped off in her hand. Feeling guilty, she stuffed it into the pocket of her skirt. "Soon it will be Christmas Eve—my birthday—and I'll still be here, imprisoned, with no friends allowed to visit, no party, and nothing to do."

"Stop overdramatizing, Rachel. You're going to school. You take your harp lessons. You had dinner with your mother last night. Listen, I was sent to my grandmother's —didn't go voluntarily—but was *sent* when my sisters had scarlet fever. And, believe me, if I'd talked to Ga-Ga the way you talk to me, she'd've washed my mouth out with Fels Naptha. She was a tyrant; at least I thought so. But your Granpa Miller, he just used to chuckle and say she was a grand old gal."

Rachel sat down on the couch next to Gram. For lack of anything better to do, she picked up the ball of fuzzy yarn and bounced it back and forth from one hand to the other. In her mind, she was trying to see backward, far enough back to when her grandmother was a girl—then a young woman married to Granpa Miller. "How did you feel when Granpa died?" she asked, her mind spinning from one image of her grandmother to another.

Her grandmother pushed her half-glasses higher up on the bridge of her nose. "Relieved. He'd been sick a long time. Turned into a miserable s.o.b., and I was glad I didn't have to worry about him anymore."

Startled, Rachel sat there wishing she hadn't asked the question.

"But I was sad, too, and I miss him. We had good years together—a lot of them—and I loved him. But, still, I was relieved, and I'd be lying if I didn't admit it."

Standing up, Rachel moved across the room to her harp. She plucked at a single string, letting the sound vibrate through the whole apartment until the tiniest echoes of its tone were gone. Next, she played a chord, followed by a rippling slide. Thoughts about loving and dying were all jumbled up inside her. Especially thoughts about her old family and her new one. "Sometimes, I wonder whether it's worth it."

"What?" her grandmother asked.

"Worth it to love people, if they're going to die and you're going to lose them."

She was drifting away from the conversation with Gram, becoming totally absorbed in her own thoughts, in her own fears. Her hands were clammy, and her whole body was beginning to tremble. She'd lost Fa. Now she seemed to be losing her mother, losing the special closeness they'd shared the last two years. She wasn't sure anymore if Ginger loved her enough. And she didn't know if Norm loved her at all. He didn't act as if he did.

Thinking hard, Rachel let her damp fingers pick through the refrain of "Greensleeves." Then, before the last sounds could die away, she jumped up and grabbed her cloak from the wooden coatrack. She had to get out where there was cool air to breathe.

Not certain of what to do or where to go, she headed for Rossi. She was still shaky and frightened. She didn't have any idea of what she could do to control these feelings. If she showed up at her house, she and Ginger would end up arguing. She didn't want to see Norm, either. Being at school with him and seeing the puzzled, disapproving look on his face was uncomfortable enough. He gave her those looks, but he never *said* anything.

As she wandered along in the park, she kept telling herself she was just out for the fresh air. The air was cold, though, and she had to keep moving to stay warm. Low, dark clouds were hanging overhead. Winter rainclouds.

Turning her eyes from the sky to the path, she found herself walking closer and closer to the bench where she'd abandoned the howling dog. Today, no dog was in sight. For a moment she stood there by the bench. Then slowly, she placed herself on one end of it, sitting quietly and trying not to shiver.

She didn't really want to be alone, but there was no one in her family to be with. Calling Michele would feel funny since the two of them hadn't done a thing together since before the wedding. "If I had my harp with me," she murmured, stroking the air with a rapid series of Bach chords, "then I wouldn't be alone . . ."

Thinking about being by herself made her turn her head from side to side to make sure she *was* still by herself. She didn't see a soul. Not anywhere on the paths around her or in the bushes, either.

What would it feel like, she wondered idly, to sit in a clump of bushes? She was not the desperate kind of person who did things like that; yet for some inexplicable reason she was tempted to try it. People who sat in bushes didn't have to be desperate, she told herself. They could be curious. Or sad and feeling sorry for themselves, as she was. Sitting in some bushes would be different, and she did like new experiences.

For several minutes, she thought it over. Then, squeezing behind the bench, she bent down and backed between the stiff, prickly branches until she had seated herself on the ground in a tight little hollow surrounded by leaves.

Wriggling about, she pulled her cloak more snugly about her shoulders and tried to make herself comfortable.

It didn't work. Twigs were jabbing into her head and back. The ground beneath her was wet and muddy. She simply didn't belong there, and she wanted out. Immediately. This was one spontaneous idea that was all wrong.

In the middle of those bushes, she was totally invisible. Almost as if she didn't exist. This thought made goose bumps pop up behind her ears. Yet, just as she was about to scramble out, she realized that she was trapped. Two people were approaching—a man and a woman. They were wearing identical blue parkas and had matching white poodle dogs on identical blue leashes. And there she was staring out at them through a bunch of leaves, feeling as weird as Sandy often said she was.

Those people who couldn't see her were obviously safe, all-planned-out people. Like Norm, but not like her bearded father, who used to come home from work at the department store and do things "just because." But that was all over now. Gone, too, was the way Fa used to yell when he was mad at her but hug her when she was his wonderful girl, his angel.

Her new family *had* turned out to be disappointingly ordinary. So ordinary that even her mother was losing her specialness. Rachel had been convinced that Norm had possibilities. She'd been wrong, and now she was surrounded by planned-out people. That thought and the awful closeness of the bushes made her want to scream. She almost did. It would have felt sensational to scare those poodle-people right out of their parkas. But it also might have gotten her hauled off and locked up some place.

So, clamping her jaws together, she crouched there until the couple was far enough away. Then, unable to stand it a minute longer, she burst out of the bushes, ignoring the ripping sounds as the twigs tore at her beloved cloak.

She was out again and free. She could move and breathe. Without stopping for an instant, she put her head down and began to run. Her sneakered feet were slapping against the path and moving forward so swiftly she didn't realize she was about to collide with someone until it was too late. Hurtling forward, she bumped into a boy on crutches. Sandy. The impact was so hard that they both went down. Sandy fell backward, hitting the ground so his cast made a dull thud and his crutches went clattering. Rachel landed right on top of him.

"Oh, help," she cried, rolling over to one side so she was sitting on a crutch instead of on Sandy. "Are you okay?"

"Yeah, I guess," he answered. Propping himself up on one arm, he used the other one to slap against the cast, which was sticking out from the split leg of his jeans. "I bet you did that on purpose."

"But I didn't even see you," she protested.

"Try telling that one to your mom and my dad."

Rachel was so relieved to find herself with Sandy instead of sitting alone in a clump of bushes that she almost felt like hugging him. She didn't, though. Instead, she started to joke around. "I'd better get out of here quick. Our parents—they'd probably accuse me of doing this on purpose so we could lie on the ground together and discuss sex." Then, looking cautiously about, she got up and pretended to be sneaking off.

"Rachel!" Sandy moaned.

"What's wrong? Scared we'll get caught together?"

"No," he told her. "It's just that I don't think—with this cast—I can get up from the ground without help."

"Mmm . . . right," she answered. "Okay, here—I'll pull

and you push." As she was helping Sandy to his feet, she found herself wondering how her own mood could have changed so rapidly. "Are you okay?" she asked Sandy.

He adjusted the crutches under his armpits. "If not, I'll sue you. Say, where did you come from, anyway? I was by myself, and then you were here, smacking into me like a cannonball. Freaky!"

Rachel thought for a moment. When she spoke, she told him the truth. "I was over there. Sitting in those bushes."

"Rachel! Cut it out!"

"Don't you believe me?"

Sandy shook his head. "You're strange, but you're not *that* strange."

"Who says?"

"I do," he insisted. "Now where *did* you come from?"

"From the bushes."

"This sounds like a broken record, Rachel."

She tugged at her cloak until he could look at the new rips with leaves and twigs still caught in them. "No, that's really where I was. See?"

"God, Rachel, sometimes you act worse than Kate— pestering people to pay attention to you. Why did you make trouble with Dad and Ginger? Can't you stop pushing everyone around?"

Rachel brushed a wisp of hair out of her face. "I don't push people. I don't mean to. Look . . . Well, do I really do that?"

"Yes," Sandy told her. "You're a real pain in the ass."

Sandy's words hurt, especially since what he was saying seemed to be at least partly true. She wanted to turn and run off. She didn't, though. She forced herself to stay.

"I've tried to be better," she told Sandy, "after we talked through the bathroom door and you told me I was too bossy. Have I been that bad?"

"Yes. You've had a relapse. A total relapse."

"Maybe you're right," she replied. Maybe all was not lost, she was telling herself at the same time. She had caused an enormous amount of trouble with her mother and Norm, but she might be able to smooth things over with Sandy. He was angry but willing to be honest about it. That was surely worth something. Worth making one more try to be part of a family.

"Look, Sandy, I was only sitting there—in the bushes—because I'm upset about our family. Mom. Your dad. Why, I don't even know if he likes me. He doesn't seem to. Meet me tonight and let's talk, please!"

"You've got to be kidding."

Rachel took hold of his arm. "I'm not. You seem to be the only one around who even cares enough to tell me what I'm doing wrong. Please. I need your help. You don't want me crawling back in the bushes as soon as you go."

She could see that she had gotten overly dramatic. Her threat was one more way of pushing Sandy as he had accused her of doing. Still, if it was going to work, she wasn't going to take it back. "Please, Sandy."

He was shaking his head, but she could tell he was weakening.

"Rachel, you know we're not supposed to be alone together."

"But, Sandy, I'm feeling *desperate*. Can you turn down a desperate person?" She hated herself for behaving this way; yet she'd done it so often that she didn't seem to be able simply to turn it off. A warm, rosy flush was rising in her cheeks. Sandy, who was looking right at her, was about to change his mind. "Don't let me down," she begged.

"Well . . ." he answered, after a very long pause. "Okay. I guess. When do we meet?"

"Tonight."

Sandy still looked dubious. "Where?"

She thought for a moment. Then it came to her. The perfect place. "How about Gram's garage? In her car? Sneak out and we'll meet there. But don't tell anybody. And don't let anybody follow you."

Nervously, he tapped one crutch against the path. "We shouldn't, you know. Even if you are feeling desperate. Even if it is important family stuff. That's what my dad says, Rachel, *not alone.*"

As he was speaking, she glanced back at the bushes. Looking at them gave her the shivers again. She had been feeling desperate then. Now, however, she was feeling a mixture of other emotions. She was disgusted with herself; yet at the same time she was excited at the prospect of meeting Sandy in Gram's car. A small smile flickered across her face. "Don't worry, Sandy," she told him reassuringly. "We won't be alone. I promise."

9

"I promised you we wouldn't be alone," Rachel said, as she and Sandy edged between parked cars toward Gram's green Studebaker. While she was speaking, she was pointing to the shadowy figure already seated in the car.

It was Walter, the blow-up plastic dummy who accompanied Gram Adele to her bridge games. He was sitting in the front seat, wearing a tweed suit and hat and staring straight ahead out the windshield.

"Oh, dynamite," Sandy said as he peered in. "You mean she just leaves him there all the time?"

"Of course. What do you expect her to do? Carry him up to the apartment every night and put him to bed?"

Sandy pressed his nose against the side window. "He freaks me out. And he does look real, you know. But those clothes. They must be forty years out of style."

"They are. Those were my Granpa Miller's clothes."

"Creepy."

Rachel took hold of the door handle and clicked it open. "Come on," she urged.

Taking his right crutch and propping it under his arm with the left one, Sandy moved toward the other door of the car. "Are we really going to get into the car, Rachel? Get in there and sit with him? That's weird."

"No, Sandy," Rachel said, getting in on the passenger side. "You've got it all wrong. We're not sitting with him. He's sitting with *us*. And it's not weird. It's funny. But it's terribly proper. We have good old Walter here to chaperone us and keep us out of trouble. And, naturally, we can count on him to keep a secret."

Sandy shook his head. "And if he tries to blackmail us?"

"We'll murder him," Rachel whispered. "Stick a pin in him and—psst—bye-bye Walter."

"Sometimes, Rachel," Sandy said, staring down at the garage floor as he spoke, "you are strange. Sometimes bossy. But sometimes you are more fun than anybody."

Rachel's cheeks felt warm. Being with Sandy was much better than sitting by herself in a clump of bushes. Pleased yet embarrassed by his words, she hurriedly changed the subject. "Are you sure you weren't followed?"

"Sure I'm sure," Sandy answered, pushing her door closed with the end of one rubber-tipped crutch. "So, move over, Walter, here I come." Then he swung himself around to the driver's side, where he opened that door and started to back in. "Hey, I can't make it. The cast won't fit and I can't squeeze past the wheel. We'll have to get out and change sides."

Laughing, Rachel and Sandy both got out of the car again, passed one another, and climbed back in on the opposite sides. Rachel was delighted with the ridiculousness of the situation as she found herself seated next to Walter, who was next to Sandy in Gram's car, which was parked in the dim apartment-house garage. To see Sandy's face, she had to lean forward past Walter and rest the side of her face against the steering wheel.

"Maybe I'll put Walter in the back seat," Sandy suggested.

"Oh no. Absolutely not. He wouldn't be able to chaperone as well back there," she said. "He might miss out on something."

As she was talking, Rachel could feel her mood changing. Already she was searching her head to determine why she'd wanted to meet Sandy. She didn't really think he could help her solve her family problem. He was, after all, part of it. Besides, what were they going to talk about? Nothing, she decided. They'd probably just sit there for a while. Then she'd go back upstairs and he'd go home. Home to *her* house.

She looked over at him. He was fiddling with one of his crutches. He didn't seem to have anything to say, either. She was beginning to perspire. She could feel wetness at the backs of her knees and between her fingers.

Determined to break the awkward silence, Rachel began to make small talk. "How's your leg?"

"Fine," he said.

"When will the cast come off?"

Sandy shot an uneasy look in her direction. It was obvious that he didn't think she was as much fun now as he'd thought only a few minutes before. "Soon," he said.

Feeling increasingly uncomfortable, Rachel dredged up another topic of conversation. "Your violets? How are they?"

Sandy grimaced. "My violets! Rachel, cut this out. You don't give a damn about my violets. I thought we came here to talk about our family and about you."

"We did," she answered, recoiling from his angry tone of voice.

"Like hell we did. This is the same old stuff. You thought it was funny to trick me. Another wild Rachel plan. Come have a happening sitting with Walter."

"But, Sandy . . ."

"Quiet. It's my turn to talk! This is not the least bit funny. I was wrong before. I've let you push me around again. We'll probably get caught, too. I bet you're even looking forward to that. How could I have been so dumb? Why don't you change yourself, instead of trying to change the rest of us?"

Surprised by his anger, Rachel's first impulse was to issue a threat. "If I don't like our new family, I can make things happen."

Sandy pounded a fist against the dashboard. "Make things happen? Why can't you just *let* things happen?"

"Because I'm not happy, that's why. Not since Fa died. It's not fair."

"Fair?" he replied, almost shouting. "Who says life is fair? Why am I so short? I *hate* sitting on the bench while the tall guys get to play. Is that *fair*? Besides, it's not true that you're not happy. I see you happy lots of times. So why do you expect it to be *all* the time? Why? Huh?"

Rachel didn't answer right away. This was a different Sandy than she had ever seen before. Not only was he willing to speak up and challenge her, but he was willing to let her see part of what was going on inside his head. It had never occurred to her that he minded being short. For the first time, she was aware of the fact that he was probably a very interesting person. Sandy, she realized just then, was someone she would like to get to know.

When she finally spoke, her voice was unusually quiet and tentative. "Sandy?"

"What?" he snapped.

"I was wrong to think you didn't know about anything except sports. You seem to know a lot about people."

Sandy sank back in the seat. He was silent. His anger was vanishing and being replaced by a different kind of emotion. Rachel saw immediately that she'd said too much. She was going about this all wrong.

Tentatively, she brought the conversation back to herself. "I do want to be better. To stop messing things up. And I'd really like you to help me."

"Sometimes I want to. But sometimes I don't," he told her.

"Like right now?" she asked, beginning to feel that their conversation was over and that she'd rather be back up in Gram's apartment reading her book. "I don't always like myself very much, either."

"Okay—well, now that you've said you *want* to change, what are you going to *do* about it?"

Rachel shrugged. "I'm not sure. Maybe there's nothing I can do . . ."

"Nothing? Nothing? What am I doing here? Why did I come? What are you thinking about, Rachel?"

"I was thinking," she responded honestly, "that right this minute I'd like to be upstairs reading *Slaughterhouse-Five*."

Sandy punched Walter, making his spongy body press against hers. "That's a good story," he said, obviously relieved to find they were about to discuss less personal matters. "Have you come to the part where Billy Pilgrim visits Tralfamadore?"

Trying to get a better look at Sandy's face, Rachel squinted. "You've read *Slaughterhouse-Five*?"

"Sure," he said.

"For school?"

"No, I just read it."

"Oh, come on, Sandy, you don't read. Ever."

Through the dimness, she could see Sandy's large white teeth gleaming at her. "There're lots of things about me you don't know. Like—do you want to know my favorite part of *Pride and Prejudice?*"

"Oh, yes, tell me," Rachel said, wondering if he was bluffing.

"I like the part where Elizabeth turned down Mr. Collins and told the stuffy bastard she wouldn't marry him."

"Well, yes—that's a good part," Rachel agreed, tapping her right fist against the steering wheel. She tapped at it so carelessly that the horn gave a little beep. "But not nearly as super as the garden scene with Elizabeth and Darcy at the end."

"No, too mushy," Sandy answered thoughtfully. "But what about the old lady? Lady Catherine—Liz's last meeting with her?"

Rachel smiled. She might still be feeling angry and uncertain about her mother and Norm, but she wasn't mad at Sandy. He at least listened to her. She'd meant it when she'd said she thought he could help her. She was ready to go back home. She'd speak to her mother in the morning.

Because she was preoccupied with these thoughts, it took her several minutes to notice that the garage was brighter than it had been earlier. A long triangle of light was slicing through it now. When Rachel did look up, she saw a man leaning against the door leading from the apartment lobby. Because the light was shining in from behind him, Rachel couldn't see his face, but she didn't need to. The squared-off shoulders and arc of curly hair told her immediately that she was looking at Norm.

Sandy was busy explaining something he'd heard his father say about Elizabeth Bennet having been a very liberated woman for her day and age. Just as Rachel was deciding she'd better alert him, the wedge of light disappeared. The door slammed, and Norm started walking toward Gram's car.

Sandy jumped. "What was that?"

"Your father," Rachel answered.

"Dad?" Sandy gasped. "I'm getting out of here."

"Too late," she told him as she began rolling down the window. She was surprised to see Norm, but not particularly upset. He always managed to avoid dealing with her. He left things for Ginger. This time, though, he was alone. He'd found her with Sandy. Now he didn't have any choice. He'd have to get angry at her.

"Hello," she called out.

It was dark in the garage, but not so dark that she couldn't see the grim expression on his face. Paying no attention to her greeting, he bent down and addressed Sandy. "What are you doing here? I thought I told you that Ginger and I want you to stay away from Rachel. Then you go sneaking out at night, and I have to run around until I find you and find out what's going on."

"But, Dad . . ." Sandy said.

Rachel stuck her head out the window, blocking Norm's view of Sandy. Norm was still treating her like a stranger. He was leaving her out again, and she felt cheated. "It wasn't Sandy's fault," she said. "It was mine. He came here because I tricked him."

Norm shook his head emphatically. "I'm not here to deal with you," he said. "That's your mother's problem. Sandy's mine. He's old enough to be responsible for his actions and he can—"

"How come you never get mad at me?" Rachel asked, interrupting. "No matter what I say or do, you don't get mad at me. Mad at other people, but not me. What's the

82

matter? Is it because I'm not your daughter? Don't you even like me enough to get mad?"

"Shut up, Rachel," Sandy said, opening the car door and beginning to swing himself out. "Is this what you call trying to be better? Aren't things bad enough without you making them worse again?"

Sandy's words made her feel guilty, but she couldn't seem to stop. "How come, Norm? How come you never get mad at me?"

"Don't I?"

"No," she told him. "You never do."

Not like Fa used to. For not practicing her harp. For talking back. For chewing on her fingernails, and a lot of other things, too. Getting mad was part of loving. From Fa—and from her mother, too—she knew that.

"You never get mad at me," she repeated.

As she spoke, Norm backed up slightly. "Okay," he said. "Okay, all right—if that's the way you want it. Why are you disobeying us and sneaking around at night? I don't want to be here, you know. I want to be home in bed. I promised your mother I'd go out photographing with her at six o'clock tomorrow morning, so I'm mad at being kept up. Now, tell me why you're here with Sandy, and make it quick."

Smiling at the way Norm was pretending to be mad at her when he was only mad at Sandy, Rachel abandoned all her good resolves. If Norm wanted to think the worst, she'd be happy to help him out. She wasn't at all sure she even cared what he thought anymore. She leaned back against Walter's tweedy shoulder. "We were talking about African violets," she said. "Whether they need mist *and* light or just mist."

"Cut it out, Rachel. And tell me—succinctly—what it is you and Sandy are doing here."

"Well, we have things to talk about. What you and Mom do when you're alone. Whether Gram Adele has a sex life. How we feel about older people being interested in sex, too . . ."

"Rachel!" Sandy yelled. "She's lying, Dad. That's not what we were talking about. We were talking about *Pride and Prejudice* and about *Slaughterhouse-Five*. You see, she's read those books, and I've seen the *movies* and—"

Rachel opened the car door. "Don't be stupid," she told Sandy. "If no one believed us when we said we were playing basketball with oranges while we sat on your bed, no one is ever going to believe we were sitting in the car in the dark trying to decide which is the best part of *Pride and Prejudice!*"

10

"Hello, Mom. Good morning. Surprise," Rachel said as her mother and Norm slipped out the kitchen door.

Rubbing at her eyes, Ginger—her camera slung around her neck—peered through the 6 a.m. half-light. "Huh?"

Rachel leaned her head to one side. "Mom, are you still mad because Sandy and I sat in Gram's car last night? Mad like you were when you called and told me I was so awful you might *never* let me come home. You didn't mean it, did you?"

As soon as these questions were asked, Rachel changed her position on the curb and looked over at Norm. "See, she gets mad at me? Why don't you?"

Norm didn't answer. Neither did her mother, so Rachel kept on sitting there, examining them through strands of uncombed hair. As she was doing this, she hoisted Gram's broom up over her left shoulder. To the broom was fastened a hand-lettered sign that said: FREE RACHEL. LET HER COME HOME.

Ginger's face registered dismay and surprise; then it became animated. Opening the camera lens to let in as much light as possible, she began snapping pictures. Moving quickly, she jumped around photographing Rachel from every possible angle.

"May not come out," Ginger kept muttering to herself. "Not quite enough light. Not quite."

Norm still didn't say anything. He just stood there, hands in his pockets, watching.

Rachel didn't know whether to laugh or cry. She'd gotten up before dawn to intercept her mother so she could discuss the possibility of returning home, and her mother's reaction was to start taking pictures. To make matters worse, Rachel was even cooperating by sitting there rubbing her cheek against the velvety edge of her cloak, when she could have been stalking back to Gram's.

What she was doing was almost automatic. So many years of being Ginger's subject had taught her to behave in the oblivious, absorbed way that made the best pictures. Now, despite her firm intentions, she was doing it again. Though she seldom admitted it to her mother, she rather liked seeing herself hung at exhibitions. Often, she thought she should get some of the credit for knowing how to be part of a good picture. All her mother was doing was pushing a button.

"Now, put the sign down," Ginger said, with a sharp whisper that cut right into her thoughts. "I want some without it."

"No," Rachel said, eyeing Norm. "I came to talk."

Ginger shook her head. "Not here," she answered, picking up her equipment bag. "We'll wake the whole neighborhood. Come along as I shoot and we'll talk as we go."

Rachel didn't bother arguing. She knew her mother wasn't going to listen. Leaving her picket sign and broom by the back door, she reluctantly started following Ginger down the street. Rachel could feel the situation slipping away from her. Already her mother was looking flushed, so absorbed in her work that she'd never want to pause long enough to listen.

Depressed, Rachel tagged along watching her mother stand, climb, and dance about in a never-ending pursuit of the perfect angle and the perfect light. Ginger, photographing, was a beautiful creature with an aura that made her seem both magical and impossibly remote. Norm accompanied them in silence.

Mumbling private bits of advice to herself, Ginger took shots of empty streets with trash blowing, of patterns of overhead trolley-bus wires, of two long-tailed doves touching beaks in a cross walk. Then, whenever she thought Rachel wasn't looking, she'd spin around and click one or two shots of her being appropriately forlorn and waif-like.

In many of the shots her mother was taking, Rachel knew she'd appear only from the back. Or maybe just one hand would show, or the toe of one sneaker crossed over its mate. She was a great subject, her mother always said, because her face and body registered dramatic changes of mood—joy when she felt good or hurt and sadness when she didn't. Someday, if her mother ever took her seriously enough, she was going to get behind a camera and be the one capturing on film all the kinds of things she understood from posing.

Right now, though, Rachel didn't feel like posing. She felt angry with her mother for using her, freezing her emotions into photographs. Not that she hadn't always done so, but today it was different. Today Rachel had very serious matters to discuss.

Still, when she saw Rossi Park ahead, she began walking toward it, engaging in a series of activities guaranteed to attract her mother's lens. First, she kicked at a beer can, then at an old, scrunched-up detergent box. After that, she tramped through a large pile of fallen leaves, causing them to swirl up around her as she moved forward. Once they were well into the park, she'd turn on her mother and force her to talk. What does Norm make of us? she asked herself, as she watched him watching her and staring at her mother, too. He hasn't said a word. She wondered if he thought—as Sandy often did—that she was a terrible person. At this moment, she felt like a terrible person, because she was afraid that before this morning expedition was over she was going to cause trouble again.

Listening to the sound of the shutter behind her, Rachel walked grimly on. After a while, she came to the bench where she'd tried sitting in the bushes. She paused, wondering how Norm and her mother would react if she got down on her knees and crawled into that leafy hollow. It was almost worth a try. But not quite. As she remembered how awful it had felt to be trapped in there, she began hurrying away from that creepy place.

Changing direction, she headed for the children's playground. When she reached it, she did the first thing that popped into her head. She bounded forward and jumped onto a swing. Standing up and gripping the cold, smooth chain links with her hands, she began to pump. She pumped and pumped, making the swing go higher and higher. Dangerously high. So high that, after a while, it started to jerk and sag in a frightening way she remembered from when she was a much younger child, when Fa would push her as she screamed, "More, more, more!"

As she got caught up in the excitement of the moment, she could feel her anger drain away. It was thrilling to be as large as she was now and hurtling that way through the air. Her cloak was whipping in and out. She was free, yet totally restrained by the arcs of the iron chain. And without seeing, she knew that Ginger was there, photographing excitedly.

Already, Rachel could visualize the blurred shots that

would take shape in the developing pans. She could see pictures of a too-big girl wearing a gleeful expression on her face while Norman Ross, her stepfather, unemotional, unfeeling, looked on.

Rachel kept pumping until her heart was bouncing around inside her chest and her arms and legs began to ache unbearably from the strain of such unusual activity. Then, as suddenly as she had jumped on and begun pumping, she stopped. Rigidly, she stood there, letting the swing go more and more slowly until, except for an almost imperceptible sideways sway, it was entirely still.

As she was savoring the stillness, her mother's voice broke the spell. "Come on, Angel. I have more than enough here. Let's head over toward Clement Street to get shots of some of the little stores before they open."

"No," Rachel answered.

"Yes, come on. Let's go."

Feeling warmth spread from her cheeks to the tips of her ears, Rachel shook her head. "No. That's enough pictures. Now I'd like to talk."

"Not now," Ginger insisted, beginning to turn away.

"Now!" Rachel said. "Please, now. Look at me. I'm here. I'm real. Can you see me here or only through the lens? You've taken enough pictures for three exhibits. Isn't it my turn now?"

Visibly annoyed, Ginger pivoted around to face her. "I knew you were being too good this morning."

Stepping down from the swing, Rachel grabbed on to one of the dull silver support poles. She was struggling to keep herself under control. "I've been at Gram Adele's for almost five days now. And I think I'm ready to come home. I'm going to be better, I promise. That's what Sandy and I were talking about last night. He's trying to help me."

89

Ginger shook her head vehemently. "I can't have you and Sandy in the same house right now. Maybe after Christmas vacation."

"I'm not going to stay at Gram's until *after* vacation. Vacation hasn't even started yet!"

Ginger slumped down on the swing Rachel had just abandoned. Her face, Rachel noticed, was tired and thin-looking. It had lines she'd never seen before and dark circles under the eyes. Even the pink cheeks had a distinctly unhealthy look when examined closely.

"It was your idea to go to Gram's, Rachel. I didn't think it would have to last very long, but now I'm not sure."

"What's different now?"

"What were you doing with Sandy in that garage? If you sneak off to some garage with him when you think none of us know what you're doing, how can I trust you back at home? What *were* you doing?"

"I just told you. And, since you don't believe me, why should I tell you again?" Rachel asked, seeing how pale Norm looked, how nervously he was scratching at the back of his neck.

"Don't answer my question with a question. Oh, Rachel, I see what's going on in that head of yours. For some terrible reason, you're trying to break up my marriage and drive Norm and Sandy out."

"I haven't been," Rachel declared. "But now that you mention it, it's not such a bad idea."

Ginger's eyes looked different, too, Rachel noticed. Sad. Bloodshot.

"Rachel, why do you want to fool around with Sandy, anyway? Aren't there boys at school?"

Staring at Norm, Rachel chose not to answer her mother. "I hate this time of year." She sighed. "Hate Christmas and remembering Fa's death and having vacation and my birthday. I don't like Gram's. I'm in her way and she's in mine. I want to come home now, close my door, and go to sleep. Maybe I'll hibernate and not come out until next year."

"That's what you say," her mother answered. "But I know you better than that. What's wrong, Rachel? Is it the Christmas concert at school? Are you nervous?"

Rachel shook her head. "I'm not nervous, because I'm not playing. I told them I didn't feel Christmas-y and didn't feel like playing carols."

"Didn't feel like it? You don't *feel* like it? Now, I want you to go back and tell them you'll play."

"I can't," Rachel said, shinnying partway up the pole and then letting herself slide back down. "It's today. I haven't rehearsed. Don't know half the chords."

"Is playing that harp only a game with you? You're talented, your teacher says. Very talented for your age. Don't you *like* the harp?"

Rachel didn't answer for a moment. When she did, her voice was unusually soft. "I'm not sure what I like right now, much less the harp. I don't know whether I like you and Norm—or myself, either. Look, Mom—listen, I feel . . . I feel confused. I feel dumb. I can't make sense out of anything. And you—you're sounding like some other kid's mother. Not like *my* mother. What's happening to you? To us?"

Instead of responding with sympathy or understanding, Ginger simply became more upset. "Rachel, why do we keep arguing? And why—tell me why you've decided to break up my marriage?"

"I haven't," Rachel protested. "I thought having you and Norm married was going to be wonderful. We'd be a whole family again. But it isn't working. We're not close anymore. You may be happy, but I'm not."

"Happy!" Ginger cried, crumpling some empty yellow film boxes between her fingers. "How can I be happy? Norm is mad because he can't stand the way we argue. You know what's going to happen? He's going to get fed up and walk out. I hated it after your father died. I was alone. Alone and afraid."

"You weren't alone. We were together. You had me."

Ginger nodded. "Yes, I did. And that helped, but it didn't fill up everything. I still felt terribly alone until— Oh, Rachel, don't you see that Norm is special? I love him. He's solid. Sensitive. Don't you see?"

What she did see was her mother's drawn, unhealthy-looking face. Shuddering, she let her eyes dart over toward Norm. *If Mom dies, Norm, do I belong to you?*

No. No. Impossible. This time, she couldn't run away from things as she'd done so many times before. She was going to have to stick it out. Fight for herself. Fight to keep her mother strong and healthy.

"Rachel, are you listening? Do you understand what I'm saying about Norm?"

"Why do you talk about him," she answered, attempting to control a quaver in her voice, "as if he's not here? Let Norm talk."

"I don't think so," Ginger said. "Right now, I'm doing the talking because I'm squeezed in the middle, with Norm mad and you mad, and you continually doing bizarre things while I'm going to pieces trying—"

"What about me?" Rachel asked, interrupting heatedly. "Don't I count?"

Before Ginger could answer, something unexpected happened. Norm stepped forward and began to speak. "Yes, Rachel, you count. But no more than anyone else. You're busy all the time like a wind-up toy that never stops. If you weren't carrying on so, we might talk seriously about what it is that's bothering you."

"I don't want to talk about anything," she said.

"Since when?" he asked. "When you're upset, you just keep talking, talking, talking, or you hide behind your harp. You don't even give in and cry like most people do."

"I never cry. Like Mom never does. Not even when Fa died."

Norm's hands were clenched into fists, and he began knocking them against one another. "Proud of that, are you? Listen, Rachel, you need our help, but you won't let us give it."

"I don't want to talk," Rachel repeated, backing away. Far enough away that she caught sight of his red socks and remembered that he was color-blind. "I think," she said accusingly, "that because you're color-blind, you see the whole world gray, instead of bright or dark like the rest of us."

Norm squinted. "That's quite an image, Rachel. And going on the offensive is always a clever way of refusing to deal with important issues."

"I just want to come home."

"If you can discuss things without all this rhetoric, I'm sure we can work something out."

Speaking in a weary, detached tone of voice, Ginger chose that moment to reenter the conversation. "She's my daughter, Norm, and this is my decision."

"Then make it!" Rachel challenged, turning fiercely on her mother.

"Maybe . . ." Ginger murmured.

"Not maybe, Mom—*yes!* I'm coming home! It's my house, too."

"We'll see," was the vague answer her mother gave.

Suddenly Rachel felt hot, burning hot. It was obvious that her mother was losing all interest in her. Ginger was beginning to choose Norm over her. She wasn't about to let her mother make that kind of choice. She was hurt. Furious. At her mother. At Norm, too, who was so cool, pretending he didn't want to shut her out and get rid of her.

Lunging forward, she grabbed hold of him. She wanted to shake him, hit him, throw him to the ground. Before Norm, her mother had never treated her this way. She wanted to hurt him, to wipe him right out of her life.

Norm stood there like a brick wall. He made no move to stop her or even push her away. Ginger tried, but Rachel had arms that were strong from moving a harp. Doggedly, she kept on flailing at her stepfather; yet he didn't budge at all. He didn't flinch or back up either as she renewed her attack.

"I hate me. I hate you," she yelled while she was pummeling him. "I hate . . . I hate . . ."

In the moment's silence that followed her half-finished outburst, she heard the click of Ginger's Rollei. Rachel's hands dropped to her sides. She started backing away. Her mother was growing more like Norm and less like her. Ginger, too, was beginning to become cold and unfeeling. Or sick. It was possible that she was sick. But, whatever, it had been happening for weeks now, only—before this instant—Rachel hadn't seen it clearly.

Yes, her mother had always taken photographs of everything. But not like today. Not like this.

Deeply troubled, Rachel continued to back away. Away from Norm, who was standing silent and frowning; away from Ginger, who was frozen behind the viewfinder of her camera.

"I'm leaving," Rachel said, speaking almost in a whisper. "For now, Mom. But I'll call this afternoon, after school. Because I must come home. Because I think you need me."

11

"Where's my mother?" Rachel asked as she opened the door at Gram Adele's and found Norm standing there. Over one shoulder she had her laundry bag and in her hand a red plaid suitcase.

"In the van," Norm said.

Ever since her afternoon phone call to Ginger, Rachel had been playing songs and carols on her harp and wondering if her mother—as she had listlessly agreed—was really going to come for her. Although Ginger had shown up at last, she hadn't even bothered to come in. Instead, she'd sent Norm to be the porter.

Rachel had been waiting alone, because her grandmother was at her regular Wednesday bridge game. Not only had she been alone, but she'd been kept waiting for so long that it had started to rain. A winter storm had blown in from the northwest, and it was going to interfere with her plans for moving home.

"What about the harp?" Norman asked, peering past her into Gram's living room. "Can I wheel it to the elevator?"

Rachel made no effort to conceal her disgruntled feelings. "No. You've come too late. If I take it out in the rain, it'll be out of tune for a week."

Despite the weather, she did want to take the harp. But she'd need Norm's help to get it into the van. If she accepted his offer, she'd have to pretend to be appreciative when she didn't feel that way at all.

"Are you sure, Rachel? It's silly but I miss the harp. I love your music, and the house seems so empty without it."

"Does it seem empty without me?" she asked.

Norm fidgeted uncomfortably. "Of course it does. That's why we're here. So come on—let's get you and your harp back home. And . . . well . . . Rachel?"

"What?"

"Hmm . . . maybe sometime—sometime you'll play a concert for me. Would you do that? I mean it, you know, when I say how much I love to listen to you play . . ."

Norm, in his awkward way, was simply trying to butter her up. She felt disgusted. She was not interested in playing the harp for him. He didn't really care about her, and she certainly couldn't imagine doing anything special to please him.

"Let's go," she insisted. "But the harp stays."

"Don't be upset," he pleaded.

"I'm not upset."

"But you are. I can see you are."

"I am not upset," she answered. "I am not upset. I am not upset."

Looking very thoughtful, Norm reached out to close the apartment door. "Sometimes," he mused, "you are a lot like your mother."

Rachel fastened her eyes on the black and gold carpet under her feet which ran down the hall, past other people's doors, to the elevator. Then, despite her anger, she spoke quietly so curious neighbors would not peek out to see what was going on.

"Don't talk to me like you know so much about me and like I belong to you, because, even though I'm worried and Mom looks kind of sick, if something happens to her, Norm, I don't know what I'll do. But I *will not* belong to you."

"Who said anything about that?"

Rachel didn't look up. "No one, but I'm telling you, anyway. You're not what I thought you'd be, not the kind of father who really cares, who'd go out at night to search for scarlet ribbons."

Norm scratched at his head. "I don't know what you're talking about, Rachel. Except that you want some sort of guarantee or proof. A contract that will assure you happiness and security. But I can't—"

Rachel pushed past him. She didn't have to listen, she told herself, since if she had her way he wasn't going to be around much longer. As he was following along after her, still making a feeble attempt to deliver a lecture, she hurried down the fire stairway and sprinted through the rain to the van. There, she found her mother, slumped behind the wheel, leafing through the morning *Chronicle*.

"Hello," Ginger said, as Rachel climbed in. She had been expecting her mother to be furious with her about the scene she'd made, but there were no complaints. Ginger looked pale and spiritless. As soon as Norm, now silent, had slammed the door and fastened his seat belt, Ginger started up the *put-put* motor and drove off. By the time they'd reached the first intersection, she was asking Norm whether it was time to have the van's oil changed.

In the back seat, shaking water out of her hair, Rachel did not feel displeased when she heard Norm answering her mother in a moody, noncommittal way. The moodier he was, the easier Rachel's job was going to be. She was determined to straighten out her life—hers and her mother's—she assured herself all the way home.

Once she was back in her house, she headed right up to her room. She was just closing the door behind her when Sandy appeared.

"Surprise," he said, stepping forward out of her closet. "Aren't you glad to be back? I'm glad. Look, my cast is off!"

She was not happy to see him, especially since he was feeling inappropriately cheerful.

"Please, get out," she said, dropping her suitcase and laundry bag in the center of the floor. "I want to be by myself."

Sandy looked genuinely disappointed. "You don't want to see me? But I waited here just to wish you happy birthday."

Rachel flopped down on her bed. "Well, you're a day too early, and I'm in a rotten mood. So why don't you get lost?"

Before he could answer, Ginger knocked and let herself into the room. "Goodbye, Sandy," she said quietly. "Run along. I'd like to speak with Rachel."

Looking embarrassed, Sandy fled. As he was slamming the door behind him, Rachel propped her head up on her elbows and waited for the shouting to begin. It didn't, however. When Ginger spoke, her voice was low and self-controlled.

"Rachel, don't say a word. Just listen to me. I've had enough of your histrionics, pranks, and so forth. Now that you're home, you are going to start to realize that you can't always have everything your way."

Ginger's voice was cracking as if she were crying or about to cry, but her wide-open eyes were entirely dry. "I have rights, too. I love you very much, but I also love

Norm, and I'm not going to allow your selfishness to louse up my life. Do you understand that?"

As Rachel looked straight into her mother's strained, too-thin face, she nodded. "Yes, I understand," she murmured.

Her mother said that she loved Norm. She probably thought she did, Rachel told herself. But she was feeling so much pain for herself, she didn't have energy left over to feel guilty about the changes she wanted to make in her mother's life.

"*Do* you understand?" Ginger repeated emphatically.

"Well, yes—but maybe it's not just me. Maybe you're lousing up your own life. You look terrible, Mom. What's wrong with you? Are you seeing a doctor? Are you sick? I don't think Norm is good for you. I think—"

"Stop it! I'm not sick. Stop talking like that. Oh, God . . ."

Rachel wanted to spring up off her bed and wrap her arms around her mother, but she was afraid to try it. She'd gone too far, said too much. Her mother was—quite obviously—sick, and sick people had to be dealt with in gentle ways.

"Mom," she said, struggling to keep her voice soft and controlled. "We'll talk later. Okay?"

"Mmm . . . yes, all right," her mother agreed. She turned toward the door. Then, pausing, she looked back. When she spoke she was addressing an entirely different subject. "Kate is coming to dinner tonight. And I want you to be nice to her. She's very sensitive, you know."

"I know," Rachel whispered tensely. She was filling up with bad feelings again. Her mother noticed Kate's sensitivity but not her own. Didn't she understand her own daughter anymore? Didn't she care? "Hey, Mom—it's me, Rachel. Remember me? I'm sensitive, too."

Ginger didn't seem to trust herself to answer. Squeezing her hands into fists, she turned and walked out of the room. Rachel was sorry for what she'd said and how she'd said it. She didn't want to make her mother into an enemy, but she knew she wasn't going to run out and apologize, either.

For a minute or two she lay on her bed not doing anything. Then she threw her suitcase and laundry into the closet. Next, not knowing what else to do, she sat in the middle of her room, hugging her chest and rocking back and forth. She wanted to go see if Demi was still around. She would have liked to hold him. Feeling his throbbing chest against her own would have been soothing. To find him, though, she'd have to leave her room. She might run into Sandy or her mother or Norm, so she didn't go.

At that moment, she was beginning to feel desperate again. Even more desperate than she'd felt when she'd tried sitting in the bushes in Rossi Park. There was a storm raging inside of her now. A storm of conflicting emotions she could hardly recognize, let alone control. All she knew for certain was that the conflict was filling her with a terrible sense of weakness and a frightening sense of power.

"I can make things happen," she told herself. "I think I can make Norm leave, but will I? Should I? What then? If Mom is sick, how sick? When Fa lost weight, it was cancer. If she is sick—really sick—don't I need help?"

Rachel was still rocking and asking herself a series of never-ending questions when Kate knocked timidly and opened the door. Looking up, Rachel saw Sandy's sister clutching a stack of books to her chest. As she stood there dressed in a wine-colored pants outfit trimmed with braid, she seemed all of a sudden like a perfect, miniature Eleanor. "Hi," she said, in her whispery little voice.

"Hi, yourself," Rachel answered, picking herself up off the floor.

"What were you doing down there?" Kate asked.

"Nothing," she answered, reaching for her hairbrush and drawing it briskly through her hair.

"I've got some new books from the library," Kate announced, holding them out in front of her. "One by Marilyn Sachs and one by Beverly Cleary."

As Kate kept on talking, Rachel stared at her, noticing the way she smoothed out her pants as she sat on the edge of the bed and how she stacked the books next to her in a straight, even pile. She was gazing at that meek little girl, seeing how she would stretch as she grew into a lean, perfect woman who'd marry and raise a family of perfect, tiny Kate-Eleanors. Suddenly Rachel felt all choked up. She could see ten-year-old Kate's life stretching out before her for twenty or thirty years. And yet she couldn't even see her own for two or three days.

"What about me?" she asked herself silently. "Will I keep playing the harp? Am I talented? Is it important? Or will I try photography? Or will I go out one day and fly off the Golden Gate Bridge?"

Oblivious to Rachel's state of mind, Kate continued to chatter. "Remember the place in *Amy and Laura* where Laura says that the most exciting moment for her is always the one *before* she opens the book? I always feel that way. Don't you?"

Rachel nodded, but she didn't say anything.

Looking puzzled, Kate leaned her head to one side. "Rachel?"

"What?"

"Don't you like me anymore?"

"Yes, I like you. Of course I do," Rachel said.

"No, you don't. I can tell. You're acting like you hate me." When Rachel didn't say anything more, Kate twisted one strand of her curly hair and kept on talking. "Do you want me to tell you what Mother said about you after she saw you at the hospital?"

"No."

"Well, I think you should know," Kate said, always looking for some chance to tattle. "She said you were a real hellion, and she was glad she didn't have to put up with you. I told Mother she was wrong—that you were nice, and I'd like to be more like you. But now I'm sorry I said that, because now you hate me."

"I don't, I don't," Rachel protested. Until this moment, she'd been holding back with Kate. But she could feel words pounding in her head. She was going to say them, too. Every last one. Not *to* Kate, but just for the sheer relief of saying them out loud. "All right—yes, maybe right now, at this very moment, I do hate you. Maybe I hate everyone—absolutely everyone, including myself. And your mother, because everything she said about me is true. But I'm going to do something about it. Stop your father from messing up my life. Your mother, if she wants, can have him back. And Sandy back, too. Because I don't want them. Would your mother like that? Would you?"

Terrified by what Rachel was saying, Kate grabbed her books and disappeared in such haste that she left her little blue shoulder purse behind. Full of a heavy, hateful feeling, Rachel kicked it under the bed, where she wouldn't have to look at it and think about Kate-Eleanors.

Then, stepping outside her door, she grabbed the hall telephone. After she had pulled it in her room and shut the door, she dialed Gram Adele's number. She was sorry that she'd been so rude to Sandy. Talking to him might have helped. But since that wasn't possible, she hoped that her prickly grandmother might come up with one or two words of comfort.

Although the phone rang and rang, no one answered. Rachel didn't hang up. Instead, she sat there, holding the receiver against her ear, listening to the empty, repetitive buzzing sound. She listened until her head began to throb. Then she eased the phone away from her ear. After that, she pushed it closer again. The buzzing got softer and louder as she changed the position of the receiver, but it was still the same empty, droning sound. Rachel sat there listening and wondering, without Gram to consult, just what she was going to have to do next.

12

"Dinner's ready, Rachel," Sandy informed her, as he pounded at her door. "We've been calling and calling. Are you all right?"

Rachel heard him, but she didn't pay any attention, because she was still holding on to the phone. She didn't want to go down to dinner. Staying where she was, she let the room grow darker and darker around her as she listened to the rain outside and to the buzzing of the phone. Finally, after a very long time, she took the receiver from her ear and pressed it down on its base.

Then she sat in her room waiting for her mother to come up and get her. To her surprise, however, Ginger never appeared. Rachel heard no sounds on the stairs or in the hall. The only noises she heard came from outside— the pelting of raindrops and the swishing of tires on the wet street.

At last, stretching stiffly, she stood up. For some reason she felt she must go down and look at them. Not join them, but linger in the dark hall outside the kitchen and watch. So, making as little noise as possible, she padded downstairs. It was puzzling to find both the kitchen and the dining room empty. Although she could hear voices, she couldn't see anyone. She felt strangely weightless, as if she were invisible, listening to the conversation of invisible people.

She found them in the living room in front of a crackling fire, dipping bread cubes into a fondue pot and laughing. They were lounging on pillows propped under them in the big white-carpeted room, which had no furniture and no artificial lighting. The only light was coming from the fireplace and from the alcohol burner under the pot of bubbling hot cheese.

"That's mine, Daddy," Kate was squealing as Rachel edged close enough to see their faces. "You stole it off my fork. That's not fair!"

Looking serious and considerate, Norm dipped another cube of French bread into the melted cheese and deposited it on Kate's dish. "Look, sweets, I paid you back. All right? No one calls me a thief and gets away with it. Now, don't you start stealing from me, or we're going to have a War of the Cheeses going on."

Leaning against the cool, wooden door frame, Rachel listened and saw the shadowy way their faces were illuminated by the fire. For a moment, hardly breathing, she stared at them longingly. The picture before her was so beautiful. This was the perfect, happy family she'd dreamed of. There they were—three curly blond heads next to her mother's darker one, which shone red in the firelight. Mother, brother, sister . . . father. The lovely scene before her looked like a painting she'd seen once in an art book.

As she gazed at them, she pulled nervously at her sweatshirt. She didn't belong to these happy, radiant people. They were having such a perfect time, too. Without her. Her mother didn't look sick tonight, either. In the dim light her face, except for the circles under her eyes, seemed almost normal. Rachel shivered. Standing there was making her feel as if she didn't exist. But she did, and it was time, she decided, to give up her invisibility.

Kate was the first one to notice as she walked in. "Oh, Rachel, you came. I wanted to get you, but you were so mean before when you talked about sending Daddy and Sandy back to Mother. And Daddy and Ginger—they said you'd come when you were ready. And look, you did. Try the fondue. It's so good."

Rachel didn't say anything. Gritting her teeth, she seated herself cross-legged in front of the empty fifth plate. Then, stabbing a chunk of bread with her twelve-inch fondue fork, she dipped it into the hot cheese. It was upsetting to hear that her mother and Norm had known she'd show up eventually.

Silently, she lifted the steamy, cheese-coated cube of bread to her mouth. The fondue itself angered her. Not because it was burning her mouth and insides, but because this kind of dinner had been her idea, and her mother had gone ahead and done it without her. Ginger had never made fondue before. Rachel had had it at Michele's house and had begged her mother to try making it. She had also begged for the firelight dinner on mounds of pillows.

Her anger was beginning to make her hot—her anger and the heat from the blazing fire. That hotness seemed to loosen her tongue. "Is this an old family recipe?" she asked her mother.

Ginger shook her head. Either she didn't notice the tone of Rachel's voice or she chose to ignore it. "No, I got the recipe from Michele O'Leary's mother, so I could surprise you tonight with the kind of dinner you've been wanting us to have."

Lies, Rachel told herself, noticing how tense Norm

looked now that she had joined the family group. A lump was swelling in her throat. If it wasn't lies, then it was a truth aimed at making her feel as guilty as possible.

Because of her mother's words, Rachel found that the food she'd swallowed was beginning to churn disagreeably in her stomach. But, to have something to do, she forced herself to keep on eating. What she really wanted was to break down and bawl right there in front of them, to show how desperately unhappy she felt. Yet, as hard as she tried, no tears came.

"Listen, Rachel," Sandy began telling her between great, gurgling swallows of milk. "Dad was just saying that if you and I liked *Slaughterhouse-Five*, we ought to read *Welcome to the Monkey House*."

Sandy was offering her polite conversation as his mother might have if she were there. He was pretending he'd read a book when he'd only seen the movie. Still, he saw that she was hurting. He cared. Not everyone, she admitted to herself, *had* to like reading books. Maybe after he and Norm had moved out—when they weren't family anymore—she and Sandy could become friends. Real friends.

"Rachel, are you there?" Sandy asked. "I said, should I pick up a copy?"

"Maybe," she answered sourly.

"Who wrote *Monkey House*?" Kate asked.

"Kurt Vonnegut."

"Is it about monkeys? Would I like it?"

Rachel didn't laugh at Kate's questions, but the others did. Sandy even reached forward over the fondue pot and tugged at one of her bright curls. "You're a little monkey," he said.

In response, Kate's face wrinkled up. "Stop teasing me.

Daddy, don't let him tease. I thought that book was about a zoo and I like zoos."

The new wave of laughter produced by this earnest, little-girl comment made Kate's eyes fill with tears. Ginger, eager to comfort her, leaned over and whispered softly in her ear. Rachel felt like grabbing a handful of Kate's blond hair and pulling it out by the roots. She was still seething when Norm—looking sober and tight around the mouth—told her he'd go with her in the morning to pick up the harp if the rain had stopped, and Sandy asked her if she wanted some salad.

"Fine," she told Norm.

"No, thanks," she told Sandy.

Although she managed to answer, her attention was focused on her anger. She was thinking hard. Thinking, planning, and waiting. After a while Ginger brought an apple pie out from the kitchen. Looking at it, Rachel knew that her moment had arrived. She let out an audible sigh. Apple pie was not one of Ginger's specialties. The burned crust indicated that this one had been made in their kitchen and not at the Danish bakery. Her mother's pies were always lopsided and rather dried-out.

The sigh hadn't gone unnoticed, Rachel realized, as her mother slid a slice of pie onto a plate and dropped that plate in front of her expressively enough that the fork bounced off onto the rug. Rachel leaned forward. "Is there any vanilla ice cream?" she asked, taking hold of the fork and starting to rake it through the long white fibers of the rug.

"Ice cream?" Ginger said, looking suddenly very tired. "You've got pie. I fixed it for you. But, Rachel, I didn't *want* to make pie this afternoon. I wanted to walk with Norm and take pictures."

"Pictures?" Rachel asked. "Take a walk? It's been pouring all day!"

"Well, that's beside the point. I still did it for you. Nothing I do is ever enough. You think you should get everything you want and more. Homemade pie isn't enough for you. You want ice cream, too."

The idyllic part of the family dinner, the part that had looked like a painting, was over. That image was destroyed, and Rachel had done it. Norm, who was looking moody and upset again, would have to see Ginger as she was instead of thinking of her as a creative genius, sweet wife, and happy homemaker. Because of the strident voices, Kate had started to sob quietly, and Sandy was pounding one hand into an imaginary baseball mitt. Norm appeared to be staring with total absorption into the dancing fire, but Rachel could tell by a slight twitching in his left cheek that he was listening intently.

"Come on, Mom," Rachel said, acting as if she were innocent of all bad intentions. "What's all this about? Why are you yelling? All I asked was whether you had any ice cream."

"I know what you asked!" her mother snapped, dumping a wedge of pie onto a plate and shoving it so brusquely at Norm that its triangular tip drooped over one edge precariously. "And I know what you meant, Rachel, exactly what you meant, so don't pull that sweet, wide-eyed look on me, because I'm not going to fall for it."

As Ginger's voice got louder, Sandy looked up. "I'll get it," he volunteered.

"What?" Ginger asked.

"The ice cream."

"No, you won't, because there isn't any. Rachel probably knew that before she asked."

Frowning, Norm responded to Ginger's comment by turning his gaze away from the fire and taking hold of her hand. Rachel cringed. Just seeing their hands touch made her feel wild. She wanted her mother back.

"Come on, hon," Norm said. "You're blowing everything out of proportion."

"Me?" Ginger yelled, yanking her hand away. "I'm blowing it out of proportion? What about her? She's my daughter, and I know her a lot better than you do. And, besides, didn't you hear what Kate said before? How Rachel said she wanted to send you and Sandy back to Eleanor?"

As Rachel listened to this exchange, she took a bite out of the pie. To her surprise, it wasn't the least bit dry. In fact, it was very good. Watching her mother and Norm annoyed at one another made it taste even better. "I like the pie," she said.

"Be quiet," Ginger told her.

"But it is good," Sandy agreed, doing his part to smooth things over.

Kate didn't say anything. She just sniffled as she sat there cutting her pie into tiny little bites.

Norm and Ginger were glaring at one another. Norm broke the deadlock. "Why do you do this to her—to Rachel?" he asked heatedly. "And why do you let her do this to you? You're still the mother around here, and she's still the daughter."

Norm tapped his fork against the edge of the plate, and for a few minutes they all sat in silence, gazing into the fire, hearing nothing but its crackle and Kate's sniffs. Then, with the anger drained from his voice, Norm started talking again. "Apple pie and ice cream," he mused, speaking as if something were caught in his throat. "I think that's a problem for all of us."

"Come on, Dad," Sandy groaned. "What's that supposed to mean?"

Norm answered, "We all want our apple pie and our ice cream. It should be enough, you know, to have one or the other. Call it the Apple Pie Theory of the Universe, if you want. Either there's only apple pie or only ice cream. Tonight, after dinner, I'll go out and buy ice cream, but tomorrow there won't be any pie left to have with it, so tomorrow we won't feel completely happy, either. We're spoiled. Did you know that? The whole lot of us."

"The Apple Pie Theory of the Universe." Sandy laughed. "You sound like a muddleheaded old professor."

"Mmm. I sound like what I am," Norm admitted, his face brightening slightly. "You know what the pie and ice cream remind me of? The dog I had—my brother and I had—when we were kids. Me—I owned the back half of the dog . . ."

"The back half?" Ginger asked.

"Right. My job was to take him—Rusty, his name was —out to do his duty. And my brother—he owned the front half. *He* fed the dog. So Rusty loved him, followed him, licked his face. And I was so jealous. I should have been happy having just what I had—part of a dog—but I wanted *all* of him."

As Norm spoke, Kate, Sandy, and Ginger had begun to smile again. They were enjoying Norm's dog story, but not Rachel. She'd had enough. Pushing the pie plate aside, she got to her feet. "Sometimes," she said slowly and soberly as she looked down at the other four, "sometimes there's no dog—front or back, no apple pie, no ice cream, and no scarlet ribbons, either!"

Norm frowned. "Scarlet ribbons? How did they get into this discussion? I let it ramble by introducing Rusty, but now you're mixing the metaphor even worse. How did we get into ribbons?"

Rachel didn't want to smile, but she could feel the corners of her mouth curving up slightly. Norm's confusion pleased her. Without answering him, she turned, walking out of the firelight and into the darkness of the dining room. There she paused, wishing her harp were home so she could sit down and pluck on it.

Since it was still at Gram's, however, she would have to spend her evening doing something else, and she already knew what. She was going upstairs. Tonight, she'd be the first one up and she'd lock herself into the bathroom with a satisfying thunk. Then she wouldn't come out until everyone else was in bed.

"Wait, Rachel," Norm called out after her. "Answer me. Tell me about the ribbons."

Rachel didn't turn back, nor did she speak. She wondered why her mother was so quiet. Probably because she was feeling sick or because she was staring into the fire, envisioning photographs yet to be captured.

Slowly, Rachel headed for the stairs. As her foot touched the bottom step, she could hear Kate's soft little voice floating through the darkness. "The ribbons are from the harp song she sings, Daddy. The one about the father who can't find them, and then there they are. The scarlet ribbons are magic, Daddy. Magic ribbons."

13

"There are no scarlet ribbons," Rachel cried, pressing the telephone receiver tightly against her ear. "Did you know that, Gram?"

Before she had locked herself into the bathroom, she had pulled the hall phone in with her so that she could spend the rest of the evening trying to reach her grandmother. It had taken a long time, but at last Gram Adele had answered.

If she heard Rachel's opening remark about the ribbons, she chose not to comment on it. "Hi, Dumpling. Happy birthday, almost. I was going to call you tomorrow, but as long as you're on the line, I can say it now."

Leaning her head back against the curved rim of the bathtub, Rachel launched right into what she had been waiting to say. "Everything's terrible, Gram. This marriage isn't working out. I don't like it at all, and now I'm trying to do something. But I need your help."

Rachel could hear knitting needles clicking. Then, finally, her grandmother spoke. "What's wrong? Be specific."

"It's Mom," Rachel said. "But it's everyone else, too. Especially Norm. He doesn't seem right for me or for

Mom. Gram, Mom looks terrible. Have you noticed? Terrible, and I'm worried she might be sick. Listen, we're not happy here. I know I'm acting horribly. But I'm feeling *desperate!*"

"Rachel?"

"What?"

"Put your mother on, will you?"

As Gram was asking to speak to Ginger, Rachel was trying to find some position on the bathroom floor that wouldn't make her tailbone ache so much. "Mom's out. They all are. Movies. It's raining like it's never going to stop and—"

"Yes, yes," Gram interrupted. "I know it's raining. I've just come home from bridge and dinner with the girls."

"They all went to the movies, and I told them through the bathroom door that I wasn't going to come. Look, please, I need your help, Gram. Need to know if I'm doing the right thing."

"Rachel, you're babbling and not making a bit of sense. You wanted to go home. You're home. Now what set this all off?"

"I want Norm and Sandy to leave."

"Just like that?"

"Yes," Rachel answered.

"You must think you're very powerful."

"I can take care of Mom—well, I might need your help, but *we* can," Rachel told her. "I can make things happen. And I can make them leave!"

"And if they don't?"

Rachel tugged at a strand of hair that had escaped from her ribbon and was hanging down between her eyes. "Why, then I'll move back in with you."

"Oh, no, you won't. Staying with me this week didn't solve a thing. And coming back won't, either."

"But, Gram . . ." The shadow-filled storm was carrying her along. She felt powerless to stop it. She was being swept along in a jumble of emotions. "Gram?"

"What, Dumpling?"

"Let me come over. Just for tonight. I feel so alone. I don't know if I'm doing the right thing. I—oh, please."

"No."

"Please, Gram. You could just jump in the car and run over to pick me up."

"No, Rachel. I'm too old to jump, and I don't want to go out alone again."

"But you wouldn't be alone. You'd have Walter on the way over, and me and Walter on the way back."

"Nothing doing. If you want to talk to me now—on the phone—fine. If you want to wait up and talk about these cockeyed ideas with your mom and Norm when they come home, even better. On the other hand, if you're furious at me, you can go ahead and hang up."

Rachel hung up. As she did this, she already knew that the phone was going to ring as soon as her grandmother could dial it. But she didn't intend to answer. She got to her feet, opened the bathroom door, and started down the stairs. Only then was she aware that her knee joints had started to feel as if they were held together with Silly Putty.

She was halfway down when the ringing started. Clinging to the walls to steady herself, she made her way to the kitchen. The wall phone there was ringing, too. She shivered as she listened to the way the bell sounds echoed off the cold white walls.

Now her grandmother was holding a phone that was ringing with no one to answer it. Listening, Rachel moved awkwardly through the unlit kitchen in search of the portable radio. The rectangle of light shining in from the hall was all she needed to locate it. She turned it on, pushing the volume knob up so high that it almost drowned out the repetitious clamor of the telephone. After a few minutes, the phone—quite abruptly—went dead, but Rachel didn't turn down the radio because she knew it would jangle back to life soon enough.

She was right. It stopped long enough for Gram to hang up and redial. Then its shrill bell sounds started up again. Trying her best to ignore it, Rachel sat on top of the kitchen table. She propped up her shaky knees and leaned her chin on them. Then, trying to blot out the frantic way she was feeling, she held the radio against her right ear and kept time to the music by tapping with her bare toes against the table's wooden top. Because of the competing racket being made by the phone and the radio, she couldn't hear the sound her toes were making, but she watched them anyway, fascinated by her futile effort to make the middle toes move independently from the others.

Finally, the phone stopped. Rachel turned off the radio and sat in the dim kitchen, letting her eyes slide aimlessly from one place to another. Slowly—very slowly—her trembling stopped as she concentrated on the proofs of her mother's photographs that were lining the formica counters. On a sudden impulse, she reached above the table and turned the switch on the hanging fixture. Light filled the room, making her squint to get a better look at the pictures.

There were many of her—playing the harp, flying off a dune, swinging on a child's swing. Something fiery and energetic showed in her face, but something sad and scared, too. That girl in the pictures, Rachel realized with a flash of insight, was quite striking. She had always avoided thinking much about her appearance, since she had always seemed so second-rate when compared to

Ginger. Yet the photos told her that she was developing her own distinctive look.

Another time, this might have fascinated her, but right now it held her interest only for a few moments. Then her eyes roamed on. There were pictures and more pictures. Even one from this morning of Rachel squaring off to pummel Norm. Her face wasn't visible, but his was. It looked extremely frightened. Getting up off the table, Rachel moved closer. She didn't remember Norm looking that way when she was hitting him, yet there it was— proof.

Next, a photo of Sandy caught her eye. Sandy on the bench. He was grinning, but his mouth looked stiff and scared. Scared he wouldn't get to play, or maybe that he would and he'd mess up. And close-ups of Kate, her eyes brimming with tears.

The dreamy, solarized wedding picture of her mother and Norm was there, also. It was mostly eyes. Ginger's face was calm, radiant, but still her almost-closed eyes seemed to be sending out a feeling of quiet terror.

Spinning around, Rachel checked each face and photograph one more time. "So, yes," she whispered, beginning to grapple with something very important. "They're all scared. Mom, Sandy, Kate—even Norm, in his closed-up way."

She examined the pictures again. A sense of self-loathing was washing over her. Yes, she could keep on tearing all their lives apart. But did she really want to do it? Of course not. And yet . . .

She felt terribly alone.

What she wanted at that moment more than anything was a companion. Not Gram. Not Sandy, either. She needed someone bigger than she was, who could comfort her wordlessly. Someone who wouldn't make her feel more miserable and more guilty than she already did.

Finally, an idea came. She knew exactly whom she wanted to see. The perfect person. She'd have to go out by herself in the rainy darkness, but it would be worth it.

Very soon, she was splashing along half-flooded sidewalks, listening to the hissing spray made by her spinning wheels. Rain was splattering into her hair, down her face, drizzling into her mouth as she opened it to take deep breaths. Being out alone in the city at night could be very dangerous, but tonight no one would bother her. No one would dare. And besides, she assured herself foolishly, coming home she would have someone to help protect her.

Instead of skating the whole way, she compromised by catching the Geary bus. As she climbed on board in roller skates and with a cloak so old and wet it was beginning to disintegrate around her, the bus driver stared at her in disbelief. Shortly, though, she escaped from his quizzical looks by climbing unsteadily out of the bus and heading straight to the place her friend would be.

As she had anticipated, he was waiting for her in his car. Smiling, she opened the door, reached in, and put one arm around him. She was not alone anymore. Now, she had a large, quiet companion to keep her company.

"Hello," she said, giving him an affectionate squeeze. "Everybody hurts. Everybody's scared. Everybody—except you!"

He didn't answer, but she didn't care. She was feeling flushed and happy. Through the lens of a nonexistent camera, she could see them both. Herself in the dripping cloak and her unusual friend in his ill-fitting clothes. Her friend. *Click.* Her friend Walter. Rachel was kidnapping Walter!

She was sorry Sandy wasn't there just then. This was one idea, one adventure he would have liked. Sandy was forgotten, though, as she began skating off down the sidewalk with Walter. It was difficult to balance his unwieldy body as the old tweed clothes got wetter and heavier. When she boarded the return bus, that driver examined her suspiciously in his rearview mirror while she tried to decide whether she should sit in Walter's lap or he should sit in hers.

It was good to have ideas, she was trying to convince herself as she dragged Walter off the bus and skated with him the two blocks back to her house. Better than sitting around brooding. Better than listening to lectures from a stepfather who talked about apple pie or who thought owning the back half of a dog had anything to do with having a happy or unhappy time growing up.

Maybe she and Walter would need showers to warm up, and a change of clothes. Maybe Walter would like to put on Norm's maroon bathrobe and get into his bed to read the papers. Maybe he'd rather put on a basketball uniform and stand in Sandy's closet, waiting to surprise him when the door was opened. Or maybe she and Walter would go down to the darkroom and sit there on the stools in the dim red light, using the enlarger to make photograms of their hands.

She was still deciding when they found themselves in front of her house. Because Walter's weight had at least doubled as the rain had wetted him down, she had to prop him up against the sycamore tree by the driveway as she fumbled for the doorkey on the chain around her neck. It wasn't an easy job, either, because Walter kept threatening to slip sideways and plop face first into the muddy, flooded gutter.

She'd just put her fingers on the key when she realized

that *they* were home already. Kate had been dropped off at Eleanor's, but her mother, Norm, and Sandy were standing in the kitchen with the door wide open. They were watching her, shouting at her. With concern. With anger. Coming home to find her missing, they'd been worrying about her. Really worrying.

Suddenly horrified by her own inexcusable behavior, Rachel dropped Walter in the gutter. Then she pulled off her skates, raced through the kitchen and up the stairway. She was ashamed to face any of them. Going out for Walter had been a rotten idea. She felt awful.

14

"Who is that man? Who is he? Get him," Rachel could hear Ginger yelling. "Go after him. Catch him. I can't stand it. Not one minute more. Rachel refuses to go to the movies with us. And why? Because she's running around at night in the dark with some strange man!"

"But, Ginger," Norm protested. "Stop shouting and look. That man lying there in the mud—that's just Walter!"

"Walter!" Sandy chortled. "Walter!"

"I don't care *who* it is," Ginger shrieked. "She was out alone, wasn't she? Wandering by herself at night without even telling us where she'd gone. So why are you laughing, Norm? And the same goes for you, Sandy!"

"But, Ginger. She's back. She's okay."

"Sure, go on, Norm, go on and grin and weasel out like you always do when there's anything serious to be handled!"

From her position on the stairs, Rachel couldn't see any of them, but she could hear them quite clearly. What was going on should have been funny. It wasn't. She should have been sprinting for the bathroom to lock herself in; instead, she was leaning against the bannister, listening and watching drops of water from her cape dribble around her feet.

"I do not weasel out, Ginger. And, Sandy, get that dummy, throw him in the garage, and go upstairs, will you?"

The pitch of Ginger's voice was getting higher and higher. "You do. And you still think it's funny, I can tell."

"Take it easy, Ginger. Sit down. You don't look well."

"I don't *feel* well!" she cried. "And I don't *want* to sit down. And I am *not* going to take it easy!"

"But, Ginger . . . hon . . ."

"Don't patronize me, Norm. It's all well and good for you to be calm and see humor in the situation. She's not your daughter. What if it were your Kate, your precious Kate, in the dark with some man?"

"It was not a man. It was a plastic dummy."

"I saw him. I know. But that's beside the point. It's the principle of the thing. She was out alone—at least as far as my mother's and back. Don't tell me that's harmless, a harmless little . . ."

As Ginger was shouting these things and others, a wordless Sandy fled from the kitchen and up the stairs. With his eyes fastened on his sneakers, he pushed past Rachel and thudded down the hall to the bathroom. Then Rachel heard the door slam and its lock click into place. She twisted one edge of her cloak and watched the water making a little red lake on the wooden boards under her feet. Now Sandy was barricaded in the only room in the house with a lock on the door. When her enraged mother came after her, she'd have no place to hide.

She wasn't sure, however, that she deserved to have a hiding place. Going for Walter had not been just a harmless little joke. There were strange people out at night.

What she had done was wrong. Scary. She was feeling genuinely ashamed for all the trouble she'd caused.

Swallowing hard, she forced herself to listen again to what was going on in the kitchen. Nothing had changed very much except that by now Ginger was pounding a chair against the floor as she spoke. ". . . deliberate! All of it deliberate! Going out at night. Worrying me with a stupid prank. Don't you see, Norm, she *is* trying to wreck our marriage. And you keep refusing to take this seriously. I don't want her to destroy everything. But she's getting her way. She's doing it!"

As Norm attempted to answer her mother's tirade, his voice was strained but under control. "I'm fed up, Ginger. Tired of hearing you come down so hard on Rachel. We don't talk about anything else—even alone—except Rachel. And it's always an argument. I'm tired of it. You know I don't like to argue."

"I'm not arguing. I'm stating facts."

"What you think of as facts, Ginger, and what I think of as facts aren't always the same. And we *are* arguing about the only thing we ever argue about—the kids and, most specifically, Rachel. It's not all her, either. I think you ought to examine—"

"Me? Me? You just sit back and get that cool professor look on your face. You sit around reading while I'm going out of my mind and not getting any work done for my exhibit next month."

"Work? For God's sake, who was talking about work?"

"You see, you don't take my work seriously, Norm. I knew you didn't."

Ginger's enraged voice was getting louder and louder, leaving the kitchen and approaching the downstairs hall. In response, Rachel turned and flew upstairs to her room. Once there, she closed the door, stripped off her soggy clothing, and wrapped herself in her terry-cloth robe. Next, she stuffed her revolting-looking cloak into her wastebasket. Then, shivering, she sat on the floor, near the door, and waited for her mother to come bursting in.

To Rachel's amazement, though, Ginger didn't even hesitate when she came past the door. Instead, with heavy footsteps she ran down the hall to her own room and slammed the door behind her. Norm's jogging steps followed her mother's. He, too, went past Rachel to the end of the upstairs hall. From where Rachel sat, it sounded as though he had thrown the door open, flinging it so hard it bounced against the dresser behind it. His voice carried to Rachel's ears in loud, distinct tones. "That's it, Ginger! If anything gets to you, you just yell, talk about photography, and run away!"

Standing up, Rachel opened her door a crack. Then the voices echoed even louder.

"Oh, hell. Go away! You don't understand anything, Norm," her mother was shouting. "If I'm so childish and illogical, why don't you take your things and get out. Take Sandy if you want—or leave him. He's no trouble."

"Ginger, I can't discuss anything with you when you're like this. Can't we start again and talk rationally?"

His question was answered not by words but by a thud and then another thud coming from the bedroom. After that a whole series of jarring, thudding sounds shook the house. Rachel shuddered, picturing an angry, bewildered Norm trying to argue rationally with her irrational book-throwing mother. Rachel was still standing there listening to the books smack against the walls, the furniture, and the floor when she realized that the bathroom door had been surreptitiously unlocked. Now, through a two-inch crack, Sandy's nose and mouth were visible as he listened in, too.

". . . and that's right—the easy way out," her mother was saying, beginning to puff from the exertion of emptying the bookcases. "Just intellectualize everything, Norm. Then nothing ever hurts. I knew we hadn't known each other long enough. I thought I loved you because you were so stable, so solid. But that's not how you are. You just seem that way because *you don't feel anything!*"

"That's some accusation," Norm commented. "And from the very woman who stops to take pictures when her daughter is beating up her husband!"

Rachel pushed her door closed. Then she slumped down on the floor and leaned against it. She couldn't bear to hear any more arguing. She felt responsible for it all. Besides, those loud voices were reminding her of something she thought she'd forgotten long ago, of other arguments. Wild emotional arguments between her mother and Fa, with both of them shouting and throwing things while she, a little cat-eyed girl, peeked around corners or hid under the bed, cringing in the dust.

She hated having these pictures stirred up out of her dim memories. Sitting there, in the dark, she found she was seeing Fa again. In the hospital bed with the I-V dripping into his arm, looking thin and bruised and old. She could hear his voice again, too, telling her that he could *make things happen.*

When had he started saying that, she strained to remember, before or after he got sick? Had he always been that way, or was that only what he said frantically as he'd felt his life slipping away? She wasn't sure. She'd only been eleven. She couldn't bring it back.

As she probed for answers, Rachel ran her tongue nervously over the tips of her fingers, looking for a jagged corner to bite. Her nails had to be filed almost to the

quick for playing the harp, and she seldom bit them anymore. Not since Fa died, at least.

Even dying, he'd still yelled at her when he found her,
fingers in the mouth, searching for that tiny, comforting
corner. Until this instant, Rachel realized, she'd almost
forgotten about the nail biting. About his terrible reaction
to it. How much more had she forgotten or simply been
too young to understand?

She'd loved him so much. But she'd hated him at the
same time. For yelling. For being about to die. If he'd
truly loved her, she'd told herself then, he wouldn't leave
her. And if *he* went away, how was it ever going to be safe
to love anyone else?

Fast, running footsteps jarred this disturbing question
out of her head. They were pounding down the hall, down
the stairs, and out the back door. It slammed. The house
shook. At the curb, the van's coughing motor started and
its tires screeched as it pulled away from the curb. When
the sound of the van was no longer audible, Rachel still
sat there listening. She sat in the dark staring at nothing.
Then she started squeezing her eyes tightly closed and
opening them wide to create little colored bursts of nothingness. As she was absorbed in doing this, she found herself talking out loud. "Norm is gone," she said, trying to
decide how she felt about that fact. Norm, who had stood
up for her tonight when her own mother wouldn't, was
gone. And she'd done it. She'd made it happen. "How do I
feel now?" she asked herself hollowly. "I feel horrible . . ."

While she was talking to herself, noises began to in-
trude on her vague sense of nothingness. One was the
sound of the shower running. Sandy must have relocked
the door. He was standing in the shower under the jets of
hot water, trying to wash all the angry loudness away.

Washing, and wondering, probably, what was going to happen to him now that his father had walked out.

Pressing her ear against the closed door, Rachel began to realize that she was hearing another sound, too, but she couldn't tell quite what. Sliding a few inches from the door, she opened it slightly to listen. What she heard then was crying. Not crying that was muffled and coming from the locked bathroom where Sandy was, but crying coming from the wide-open bedroom at the end of the hall.

What she was hearing was a hoarse, horrible sobbing— full of suffering and real desperation. Listening to it made her shiver with fright. Never had she heard her mother cry. Not all the time her father was dying or when he died, even. All of her mother's emotions spilled out of her mouth instead of out of her eyes. But now that Norm had left, her mother, for whom Rachel had been feeling such hate, was down at the end of the hall alone. Alone and crying out in a way which was so terrible it made waves of goose bumps flow across her scalp and down her arms.

Slowly, forgetting her own pain, Rachel stood up. She wanted to run and hide again, but this time she wouldn't let herself do it. She didn't know what she'd say or do when she got to her mother's room, and yet she knew she had to go. It was all her fault . . .

At the threshold of the room, tugging at the ends of her bathrobe belt, she paused. She was still standing far enough back that she couldn't see in yet. "Mom," she called softly. "Mommy?"

15

"Mommy?" Rachel repeated, still hesitant about entering the room.

"Go away!" a hoarse voice croaked.

Stunned, Rachel leaned forward and peered in. The sobbing figure sprawled across the bed wasn't her mother at all. It was Norm. For a moment, Rachel stood there staring at him, trying to decide what to do. She was tempted to go away just as he had told her to do. In some ways it would have been easy to pull the door closed and turn her back on the sight of a full-grown man crying out in such a frightening way. Still, she couldn't make herself leave.

"Norm?" she asked, moving a few feet forward.

He didn't answer. She really hadn't expected he would. His large, square hands were over his eyes, and as if she weren't even there, he continued to cry. Feeling the need to do something useful, Rachel picked her way across the book-strewn floor toward the bathroom. There, she took a hand towel, soaked it in cool water, and wrung it out. Delaying the next step, she squeezed and squeezed at the towel. When she had reduced the excess water to the smallest possible dribble, she walked back through the bedroom to where Norm was lying. Then, without a word, she placed the towel over his forehead and eyes.

As soon as she had done that, she sat on the floor next to the double bed. After thinking about it for a minute or two, she reached out and took one of Norm's hands into both of hers. She sat there so long like that that her neck got stiff and her right leg fell asleep all the way up to the hip joint, but she didn't move. She didn't want to disturb Norm, who was gradually beginning to regain his self-control.

Finally, in a voice that was trembling and so low it was almost inaudible, he spoke. "Thank you," he said.

Nervous and embarrassed, Rachel drew her hands away from his and sat on them. "Don't thank me," she mumbled. "It's all my fault . . ."

"Some of it," Norm said, beginning to wipe his face with the damp towel she'd brought.

When he finished with the towel and dropped it down next to the bed, Rachel picked it up and sent it flying through the air into the bathroom. Next, she forced herself to ask Norm some of the questions which were weighing her down. "What's going to happen? Are you moving out? Will you get a divorce?"

"A divorce?" Norm said, sitting up abruptly. "Is that what you think? Your mom and I may not have known each other very long, but we love each other. Do you really think I'd let her get away that easily? Or you either, for that matter?"

"Then why were you crying?"

"Despair," he told her. "Fear. Sadness, because people can do and say such crazy things to hurt one another. I was crying because—but you're the girl who never cries. Do you have *any* idea what I'm talking about?"

"Some of it," she responded, wondering why it hurt to

hear herself called the girl who never cries. She'd always been so proud of that. Well, everybody hurts, she reminded herself silently. Norm, too.

Then, turning her head so she wasn't staring at his swollen eyes, she saw that Demi was edging his way around the door and slipping into the room. This was the first time she'd seen him since she'd returned from Gram Adele's. He hadn't wandered off, after all. Coming closer, the cat rubbed against her knees and proceeded to settle himself in her lap. She was glad to have him there. She liked feeling his silky warmth, liked being able to use her fingers to stroke under his chin.

"Listen, Rachel," Norm said, as she was tickling at Demi's black and white whiskers, "neither you nor Ginger is going to get away from me. Any more than I'd give up Sandy or Kate. I'm not going to get a divorce. How stupid do you think I am?"

His voice was strong now, firm and irritable. Although Rachel was listening to him carefully, she didn't look up or attempt to reply. With her shoulders slumped slightly, she continued slowly and rhythmically to stroke the cat.

"It may be hard to believe," Norm told her, "but I like having a pair of dynamos around. Still, I wonder, maybe you don't know, either of you, how you radiate energy. Sometimes happy, sometimes desolate, but so full of life that you make the rest of us jealous. Do you know what I mean?"

Surprised by his words, Rachel turned her head just far enough that she could catch a glimpse of him from the corners of her eyes. "I know, I guess. It's there in the photographs. And it's sort of like what Sandy said once. He called me Wonder Woman. Told me I had weird, fiery powers."

"He did? Sandy said that?"

"Well, not exactly. He said I acted like I *thought* I was Wonder Woman."

"Well, sometimes you only act that way, but sometimes you *are*. So we tell you those things, Rachel, and you know what?"

"What?"

"You don't trust any of us. You try to run our lives. Every silly irrational thing you do is a cry for our help. Like going out tonight for Walter!"

"My father always told me that I had to make things happen. That if I didn't, no one would."

"Oh, wonderful. Terrific. You use your dead father's words as an excuse for pushing everyone around. Look, I don't want you to be some kind of zombie. I want you to keep your sparkle, your spark of originality. But it would be nice if you'd forget all that frenzied behavior."

"I hate myself when I'm that way," she lamented. "I promised Sandy I'd be better, wouldn't be so bossy—"

"Promised Sandy? Why make promises to him? Try making a few to yourself. And when—can you remember when your father told you you had to make things happen? What was going on then?"

Rachel tensed, then said the first words that popped into her head. "You're not related to me, and I don't have to answer questions like that!"

"Oh, you don't, don't you?" Norm said hotly. "You'll do almost anything for attention, yet every time we get close to what's bothering you, you dodge and hide and change the subject. The angel vanishes and the demon appears. And then—don't tell me because I already know—in a minute you're going to be asking me for guarantees again, preferably ones written in blood."

"But—" Rachel began.

Norm didn't let her get one word further. "Quiet!" he

shouted. "I'm talking now. So your father died. Well, so did mine. And my mother. And my brother—in Vietnam. I wasn't as young as you, Rachel, but I lost them all. That's why my living family is so precious to me.

"But let's examine *the* question. If your mother dies, do you belong to me? *Yes,* if I have anything to say about it. *Yes. Yes, of course.* Does that make you feel better? I doubt it. Because, to use one of your favorite metaphors, there simply isn't any way miraculous scarlet ribbons can appear to warm the aching heart of a daughter!"

Rachel felt cold and sweaty. What he was saying wasn't all true, but much of it was. "I still don't think I want you here," she declared nervously. "It's not good. And my mother—I think she's sick. She looks sick."

"Well, she's not. She's fine. There's nothing wrong with her that couldn't be solved if we stopped putting such a strain on her."

"But—"

"No buts," Norm said, interrupting. "You are, when you want to be a demon, a little monster. Admit it. Besides, I think you like feeling sorry for yourself because your father died. You could do it again if your mother were sick, which she isn't. You *like* ordering us around, and—no matter what you promised Sandy—you don't intend to give it up. It's like Kate playing dollhouse, only you insist on doing it with *real people!*"

"No!"

"Yes! And it's a rotten game, because if things are less than perfect, you get scared and spoil them. Admit it!"

Vehemently, Rachel shook her head. "No, no—I don't spoil things!"

With his red-rimmed eyes half swollen shut, Norm glared at her. "Don't you? Isn't it easier than taking risks? Than loving someone you might lose?"

She was furious at him; yet despite her fury she suddenly realized something. "Hey . . ."

"Hey, what?" he snarled.

"You're mad at me. At *me!* Really mad at me."

"You better believe it."

Because Norm didn't say anything else, she was silent, too. Catching sight of the scattered books, she began scooting around, closing them, and stacking them up in a tall pile.

Norm was angry with her. Angry because he cared. In fact, everything he'd said showed how much he cared, how well he understood her. When she glanced over at him, she could see that he was looking very gloomy, almost as if tears were about to start flowing again. She felt angry, too; yet she wanted to be helpful, because something important had just happened. Finally, he had yelled at her, shouted at her with a voice filled with genuine emotion.

"Mom will come back," she told him. "And when she does, she won't be mad."

"I know," Norm answered, "but maybe I will."

"Will what?"

"Will still be mad. Your mother is just about the best thing that ever happened to my life, but when she starts shouting—or you and she both—it drives me to distraction. Don't make that mistake, Rachel, the same one your mother makes sometimes, of thinking I can't be quiet and furious at the same time."

Listening to him, Rachel put one more book on the stack. That made it too high. The whole pile swayed, caved in, and the books thumped against the floor again.

"Well, you're not perfect, either. If you plan to stay with us, be family instead of a Visitor. If this marriage—

our marriage—is going to work, you might have to learn to put up with *some* shouting . . ."

Norm glared at her. "Orders, orders. Always giving orders. Who says I have to put up with shouting? As for your mention of 'our marriage,' I won't even comment on that."

"Norm?" Her voice was tentative. She was sorry for her last outburst.

"What?"

"Don't be mad at me anymore. Please. Haven't we had our argument?" she said. "When Mom and I argue and it's over, we make up. Can't you and I make up now?"

"Kiss and make up?" he answered, speaking in a calm yet cold voice. "No, I'm afraid it's not that easy, Rachel."

"Why not?"

"Because . . . I still feel angry. And because you're not willing to consider why your father said that you should make things happen."

Rachel stood up. Instead of looking over at Norm, though, she stared down at the floor. She was beginning to realize something. He—Norm—wasn't shouting at her anymore, but he *was* just as mad. For the first time, she was understanding, in some still-unfocused way, that a person didn't have to yell like her mother or Fa to be angry, really angry. Or to feel love . . .

She wanted to do something for Norm. To show how much she appreciated his caring. A small beginning. "I'll play my harp for you tomorrow," she offered. "You asked once . . ."

"No," he said.

"Why not? Oh, please."

"If you really want to play it, do it for yourself. That damned harp. When we try to help *you*, the most you'll ever do is let us *help move it.* I don't think you care about it except for its nuisance value. And you certainly don't listen when I tell you—or any of us tell you—how wonderful it sounds when you play."

Slowly, Rachel was beginning to understand something. Norm meant it when he told her he liked hearing her play. Fa, on the other hand, had always commented on the way she looked behind the harp and not on how the music sounded. This was a difference between her father and Norm. One of many. Not all differences were bad.

She wanted a fresh start, but she didn't know where to begin or what to say. What she was about to suggest seemed terribly inadequate, but just then it was all she could manage. "Oh, Norm, I have been awful. But I *am* going to be better. To Mom. To you. So, can't we declare a truce?"

He frowned. "Truces can't be declared. They have to be earned."

Rachel took a deep breath. Knowing Ginger wasn't physically ill, knowing she could change and that she could help was making her feel a little better. "Yes, Norm . . . yes, I *will* try to earn it . . ."

Rachel glanced at her watch. It was almost midnight. If her mother didn't come home or if Sandy didn't unlock the bathroom door, she wouldn't have anyone to wish her happy birthday. No one—not even the kind of tender, complex person who'd settle for owning the back half of a dog. She didn't want to leave the room. She didn't know why Norm hadn't answered her last statement. "I *will* try to earn it," she repeated, speaking emphatically.

"Lip service," he growled, dismissing her with a sweeping gesture of one hand. "I'm tired of lip service. Actions speak louder than words. Now, go on. Get out. Leave me alone."

16

"Happy birthday, Angel," Ginger whispered, knocking softly and letting herself into Rachel's room. "I know I said it last night, but I wanted to tell you again this morning."

Rachel's whole body felt prickly, its assortment of arms and legs twisted up in the patchwork sheets and comforter. Tentatively, to greet her mother, she opened one eye. Then, letting it close again, she lay there remembering last night's argument with Norm, remembering, too, how relieved she'd felt when, at last, her mother had come home. Now it was morning already, even if Rachel felt she hadn't been in bed nearly long enough.

Ginger was tiptoeing around the room, raising the shades, coming over to her bed. Then, sitting down on the edge, she began to run her fingers through the long, fine strands of Rachel's hair.

Not moving at all, Rachel lay there with her eyes shut, thinking about how she and her mother had hugged and hugged one another. How she'd apologized for two months of outrageous behavior, declaring over and over again that she had no intention of trying to break up her mother's marriage. It wasn't enough, she reminded herself, because—as Norm had said—truces had to be earned. Yet, it was a start.

"How did it get to be my birthday again?" she asked herself. "How did I make it all the way to fourteen?"

Because she didn't have any answers, she kept on thinking about the questions, until she'd had enough of feeling special and having her head stroked. Then she rolled over on her back and opened her eyes.

Lying there, she examined her mother, who was looking thin and tired but not, Rachel could see now, sick. Ginger was gazing absentmindedly out the window, looking through the banks of heavy clouds in search of some slight beam of sunlight. On her face was a frown, which made a number eleven between her brows. It looked as if her mother was trying to decide if the storm inside Rachel was truly subsiding as she wondered the same thing about the larger one outside.

In answer to that unasked question, Rachel said, "I'm not making any promises or guarantees. But I'll try. And I *don't don't don't* want to break up your marriage!" Despite her words, Rachel felt fearful, worried that she wouldn't be able to carry through on them and make them meaningful.

"What?" Ginger asked vaguely.

Kicking her too-hot feet loose from the bedclothes, Rachel rolled over on one side. "What were you thinking just now?"

"About us," her mother said. "About how I love you and Norm. Sandy, too . . ."

Rachel propped herself up on one elbow.

"And Kate. About whether things would have gone more smoothly if Norm and I had waited longer before we were married."

"I doubt it."

138

Ginger nodded thoughtfully.

"Mom, listen, Norm loves you. I love you. Everything will be all right, I think. But still, no promises or guarantees."

"You're sounding like Norm," her mother said.

"I know," she agreed, thinking and remembering. She wanted to admit that last night she'd seen the kind of loving tenderness that made her mother love Norman Ross. But it seemed too difficult, too personal to say aloud, so she asked some questions instead. "What about Norm? Will he ever forgive me?"

Ginger leaned her head to one side. "Mmm . . . I suppose. It may be a while, though. Right now, he's still furious."

Thinking about her mother's discouraging words, Rachel sank back against her pillow. "Well, maybe the best thing about being mad and arguing," she said, after a long pause, "will be the making up."

"Mmm . . ." her mother murmured, as she was turning to look at the clock on Rachel's desk. "Oh, help! It's almost ten and your birthday, and I've got to get organized."

"Why?"

"Well, don't you want a party? A Christmas Eve birthday party with us? And some friends, if you want. We'll have to get our tree and decorate it. Make calls, buy food. How will I ever get that together in one day?"

Rachel was listening, but at the same time her thoughts were drifting. She wanted to hold on to all of her new resolves. Still, inside her head, an idea was taking shape. "Wait," she said, turning and letting her feet dangle over the edge of the bed. "Listen, I have a suggestion. A terrific suggestion."

"What?" her mother asked, beginning to look suspicious because of Rachel's burst of energy.

"Let's have a surprise party!"

"Huh? Come on, Angel. How do you give a surprise party for yourself? That's silly."

"No, it's not," Rachel insisted, standing up and starting a series of vigorous stretching motions. "I mean—look, with a few well-placed hints we can get the family to give me a surprise party. Then you and I could take off for the day. I haven't done any Christmas shopping. If we could get that finished, maybe we could see *Gone with the Wind* again. And go to the beach afterward to watch the sun set. Or if it's raining, we could sit in the van and watch the clouds blow in off the ocean until it's time for the party. Then we'll come home, and everyone will jump out and say, 'Surprise.' "

"Maybe," Ginger said, but her puzzled number-eleven frown was beginning to appear again.

Rachel dropped her hands to her sides. She was a failure. She'd already let herself get carried away again. "No, forget it," she declared. "I don't want to plan other people's lives. It's a bad idea. And Norm—Norm's furious, and he probably had his own plans for the day. Mmm . . . maybe I'll skate over to Rossi and look for that lost dog. If I brought him to Norm, then he could have a whole dog— front and back both."

"Absolutely not," her mother said. "What we do not need today is a dog."

Rachel twisted her hands together. Norm had said she should forget the frenzied behavior but without losing her spark of originality. It was going to take time, she realized, to be sure of the difference. "Right. No dog. But other things, and I should do them all. I'll surprise everyone else."

"Why?"

"Because I should. Because I shouldn't keep winding all of you up in my plans and—"

"But I want to!" her mother insisted. "There's too much for you to do alone. And, whatever you do, I want to be part of it. Always."

"Sure?"

"Sure I'm sure."

"After all I've said, Mom, and all I've done?"

Ginger nodded. "You're my girl, aren't you?"

Rachel smiled. Her mother had been depressed, had been angry with her, but she had not forgotten how to offer love or forgiveness. "Yes . . . yes, I am. All right then, I'll do most of it, but we'll work together. Okay?"

"Okay. So, what else? What do we need to do?"

"Well," Rachel replied, concentrating so that she would not get carried away again. "I'll pop corn and string cranberries. Borrow Sandy's violets to decorate the mantel. See about the harp. Buy pies and ice cream . . ."

"Is that *all*?"

"No." Rachel hesitated for a moment, because she had something else she wanted to say. Something silly. "Mom —wouldn't it be wonderful if Norm went, bought red ribbons, and piled them on my bed all the way up to the ceiling?"

"Cut it out," her mother said, falling back into the familiar pattern of sounding slightly exasperated with her. "What am I going to do with you? You always want too much."

Nodding, Rachel leaned back against the edge of the desk. Yes, she did want too much. And that was a major part of her problems. With her feet close together, she stood wiggling her toes, looking down at them and at the striped towel around her.

The towel brought back a long-forgotten picture. An image of her healthy, bearded father coming home from the department store with his pockets full of striped candy sticks. Then, swiftly, that image dissolved and new ones floated into focus. Pictures with a comfortable blend of sunlight and shadows. Pictures of herself making things happen. Suddenly her head was bursting with them. But just as suddenly she realized something.

Something Norm had wanted her to figure out. *Make things happen* was a statement of desperation. Her father hadn't always been that way, always recommended being that way. That had been his reaction to sickness and fear. From her shadowy memories, she drew out—at last—a different image of Fa. A joyous but calmer person. Not so very different from the kind of person she'd like to be. One who could keep a spark of originality but *let things happen.*

Besides, she was still going too fast. What she wanted—that close-knit new family—would probably come about. But it would take time. She could love them all and be loved in return. She could earn love as she found out how to earn forgiveness.

"Rachel!" Ginger said, beginning to shake her. "Come back from where you are."

Impulsively, Rachel snuggled up next to her mother. Although it had taken her weeks to understand, she was starting to see now that her mother could be close to Norm without leaving her. "I need to be alone. To think. About Fa. About Norm. About me—and us. So, forget me, and say what *you'd* really like to do today."

Ginger wrapped her arms around Rachel but held her loosely so they could look at one another. Ginger's eyes were moist, yet no tears welled up and fell.

"Your tears must all drip down inside instead of out," Rachel said. "Aren't you ever afraid you're going to start to rust?"

"Yes," Ginger admitted, holding her closer. "What about you, though? You must be rusting inside, too. And if Norm were here, he'd tell you that was a very good image."

"So tell me, Mom," Rachel repeated, whispering into her mother's ear, "what would you really like to do today?"

Ginger's answer came quickly. "Be with Norm. Have some talking time, healing time, for just the two of us. Walk across the bridge maybe."

"Then do it," Rachel insisted, pulling away and stepping back. "And don't worry about me. Or about dinner, either. I'll throw something together."

Rachel wanted to earn her mother's forgiveness as well as Norm's. Her head was spinning. Needing a quiet place to think, she peered into the hall to see if the bathroom was empty. It was. "Have fun, and I'll see you later," she said, starting to let her body spin like her head. "I need time. No guarantees. But dreams. Dreams that might happen if I don't go too fast. Maybe I'm not a total failure. Maybe I have possibilities!"

As she was talking and pirouetting, she bumped into Sandy. He had just stepped out of his room and was standing there examining her. He was sleepy-looking, but not too sleepy to notice she wasn't wearing anything but a towel.

"Don't run for the bathroom," she chirped. "It must be my turn sometimes." As she said this, she stopped long enough to plant a chaste, sisterly kiss on his cheek.

Muttering to himself, he wiped it away.

"Don't," Rachel cried out. "Wonder Woman has just touched you with her fiery powers. And now she's going to lock herself in the bathroom and wash her hair!"

"Aw, shut up, Rachel," he said, sounding embarrassed rather than irritated. "You're not making any sense."

"Shut up, yourself," she replied pleasantly. "Who wants to make sense?" She pivoted slowly into the bathroom and locked the door behind her.

17

"Take it easy," Rachel reminded herself as she finally unlocked the bathroom door and headed back to her room.
Opening her closet, she rummaged around until she found
the white gauze dress she'd worn for her mother's wedding. As she was pulling it over her head, while she was
tying a ribbon in her hair, she was beginning to plan out
her day.

By the time she emerged fully dressed, she found that
Norm and her mother had already gone out. Feeling
happy to be alone, she wrapped one of Ginger's old
aprons over her good dress. Then she quickly vacuumed
the fluffy white rugs. Next, she collected all the pillows
and candles in the house and arranged them in the living
room.

When she was shoveling ashes out of the fireplace and
preparing to put in new logs and kindling, Sandy appeared. "You look like the White Tornado. What're you
doing?"

"It's a surprise. I can't tell," she said.

"Can I help?"

She shook her head. "Thanks, but no thanks," she told
him. "There's not much to do, and I'll manage."

Sandy surveyed the living room. "How long is this
going to take you? Are you going to meet us later?"

"Where?"

"Up on the bridge. About three-thirty. Ginger said you and Kate and I should meet them by the south tower."

Rachel took a minute to think it over. Then she smiled up at Sandy. "Don't wait for me," she told him. "I have something I'm thinking about. Something of my own I may do this afternoon."

To her relief, he didn't ask her any questions, nor did he criticize her behavior. With a friendly wave, he simply backed up and left.

Singing softly to herself, Rachel proceeded with her work. She emptied out an upstairs bookcase, dusted it, and dragged it downstairs to the living room. Then, with care, she transferred all of Sandy's African violet plants from the hall bathroom to the bookcase. After misting them with the plant sprayer, she arranged them on the shelves in the shape of a pyramid. When she was finished, they gave the effect of being a leafy green tree decorated with dark pink and purple ornaments.

A search through the basement produced a string of Christmas lights with a series of tiny white winking bulbs. By winding them around the pots, she finished creating the illusion of a holiday tree. The final effect, she thought, was both simple and original.

Deciding that the household tasks were done, she took her Christmas money, put on her roller skates, and headed for the grocery store. There, she bought salami, cheese, French bread, and ice cream. She didn't stop at the bakery because she felt apple pies were not necessary. This Christmas Eve dinner didn't have to be perfect, she decided.

As she was unpacking the food, she debated whether she should try and reach Michele or a few of Sandy's basketball teammates. No, she ended up telling herself.

After vacation, there would be plenty of time to make friends with Michele again. That would be soon enough, too, to see how Sandy felt about her getting to know some of his friends.

Take it easy, she kept reminding herself as she got ready to head for her grandmother's. Despite a layer of fog overhead, she was happy to see that the sky held no threat of rain. She knew now what she was going to do with her afternoon. She hoped it would be original without being frenzied.

"Gram, I've come for my harp," she said, when the apartment door swung open.

"Just you, Dumpling. Alone?"

"Just me," she replied.

"But how will you do it? It always takes two people to move that instrument. And you know I can't be expected to do it."

"Of course not," Rachel told her, picking up a silver knitting needle from the floor and sticking it through her grandmother's hair next to the blue one that was already lodged there. "Don't worry."

"Are you sure?"

Rachel gave her grandmother a little squeeze. "Sure I'm sure. Oh, yes—and you're invited for dinner. Is seven okay?"

Gram Adele glanced down at her watch. "It's two-forty now and—"

"Two-forty already?" Rachel gasped. "I've got to go. I've got an appointment."

"And you're really taking that harp alone?"

"Yes," Rachel replied.

Looking very skeptical, Gram Adele held the door for her as she wheeled the harp out toward the elevator. Only a minute or two later, she had it down on the sidewalk. Although she didn't exactly have an appointment as she'd told Gram, she did know where she and the harp were going. She had been planning to push the harp the whole way. Suddenly, though, that was beginning to look like an overly ambitious undertaking, so she decided on another course of action. She wheeled the harp as far as the busy corner of Anza and Park Presidio. Then she set its brake and stepped off the curb.

It took a very long time, but at last she managed to stop a cab. The driver rolled his eyes around and around when Rachel told him what she had in mind.

"But we can do it, can't we?" she asked him. "I know how to fit the harp into a car. It's not easy, but with two of us we can do it. We'll need a strap for the door, but I'm sure you have one. Right?"

Again the driver rolled his eyes. He took out a handkerchief and mopped his forehead. "It's Christmas Eve," he said. "I'm driving along minding my own business and a girl in a white dress with a harp hails my cab. I think this isn't really happening."

"Oh, but it is," Rachel assured him.

The driver shook his head. "In that dress and with that harp you—"

"Yes," Rachel said, interrupting. "I've heard that one before—I look like an angel. Well, I'm not. Do you see any halo? I'm no angel. Ask my family. Now, will you take me where I want to go?"

Still mumbling to himself, the driver helped Rachel ease the harp into the back of the cab. The door that wouldn't close was secured by a strap produced from the trunk. Then, they set off for their destination.

"Say—" he said as they were driving along, "you have any money?"

"Not much," she told him. "I spent most of it on salami, but I can pay. Don't worry."

He did worry. Even after they had reached the parking lot and he had helped her slide the harp back out of the taxi, he looked concerned. Even after she had paid and tipped him, he looked dubious about leaving her there.

"It's okay," she kept telling him. "Fine. I'm not from outer space, and I'm not crazy. It's just that I've got a concert to give. It is Christmas Eve, you know."

Rolling his eyes and wiping his face again, he reluctantly backed into the driver's seat and drove off. Rachel was giggling. She was trying to imagine him telling his family about the girl with the harp who had wanted to be dropped off in the parking lot of the Golden Gate Bridge.

Once she was alone again, Rachel started skating and pushing the harp along in front of her. From the parking lot to the walkway of the bridge was an uphill climb on skates. On skates and with an eighty-pound instrument, it was an almost impossible incline. Stopping, Rachel took off her skates, tied them together, and slung them awkwardly around her neck. Then, trying to ignore how cold her feet felt against the cement, she applied all her strength to shove the harp up toward the south tower. Some people made remarks and laughed. She shut them out by running musical scores through her head.

As she was struggling along, Sandy appeared with Kate. He didn't make any remarks about how strange it was to find her up on the bridge with her harp. Instead, he offered to give her a hand.

Rachel shook her head. "Thanks, but no thanks. I'll do it myself."

Sandy seemed to understand, but he also seemed to know she was never going to be able to handle the harp alone. After urging Kate to run on ahead, he simply

grabbed the front of the harp, and silently he helped
Rachel pull it across the sidewalk. When, at last, she
nodded to indicate that she had reached her destination,
Sandy let go of the harp and ambled off without looking
back.

Though panting with exertion, Rachel still felt full of
determination. Carefully, she unclamped the wheels from
the instrument and put down her skates. Then, leaning
back against the iron railing of the bridge, she tilted the
harp onto her right shoulder.

Billows of afternoon fog were blowing in through the
Golden Gate, too much fog for the sun to be visible, yet
there was an eerie winter glow to the air which turned her
dress almost candlelight yellow. That was the last detail
she noticed before she started to play.

Concentrating, she began to perform her repertoire of
songs and carols. The wind pulled at her hair and at her
dress. It turned her cheeks and the tips of her ears bright
pink, but she wasn't conscious of any of this. All that
existed for her just then were the chords of her harp and
her own voice singing out in accompaniment. Pedestrians
began to gather in a hushed semicircle around her. Cars
slowed down to catch a few notes. Rachel hardly saw
them. She was filled with her music, with the sound and
feel of it. "What Child Is This?" "Silent Night." "Greensleeves." "We Three Kings." "Adeste Fideles." "It Came
Upon a Midnight Clear." "O Tannenbaum." Scarlet Ribbons." "Away in a Manger."

Even when she didn't know all the chords or all the
words, she went on. She was performing almost as if she
were in a trance. That was probably why it took her so long
to realize that Norm and her mother had joined the audience clustered around her. They were standing nearby and
had their arms around each other. Sandy and Kate must

have been there, too, but Rachel didn't see them. With increased fervor, Rachel played on, aware that, for once, she felt no stabbing jealousy at seeing her mother and Norm touching one another. She sang another carol and another.

Finally, after one last verse of "Silent Night," she placed her fingers against the sounding board of her harp and stopped. Slowly, wordlessly, her audience began to drift away. Rachel's head was resting on her harp. She was played out, sung out. After a few minutes, she forced herself to look up. Her mother and Norm were still standing in the same place gazing at her.

"Angel," Ginger whispered. "Your father would have loved this."

"Yes," she said, aware that this Christmas Eve was filled with both sunshine and shadow. "But I was playing for *all* of my family."

A huge lump was swelling in the back of her throat. "For you, Mom, and for someone who said 'Yes,' who wanted me to play a concert. My . . ." Here her voice dropped to a rasping whisper. ". . . Christmas gift to everyone."

As Rachel spoke, her chest began to heave with sobs. At first, there were no tears, only great wrenching sobs. Soon an unfamiliar sensation came over her as warm tears streamed out of her eyes and down her wind-burned cheeks. She made no effort to hold them back. She simply sat there crying for all the pain she'd caused, but crying, too, with relief, because she'd begun to make amends.

With no sense of shame or need to apologize, she cried until the tears stopped flowing. Then, struggling to control the lingering sobs, she began to clamp the wheels on her harp. She had tried to earn some small measure of forgiveness from her family. Tried to do something special for them. Her mother and Sandy and Kate were pressing in close to her. She could see how they felt. But what about Norm? Instead of moving toward her, he was moving away. Turning, he suddenly began striding off without a word.

Rachel knew it would be no use to run after him.

Had she really played for her family? Or for herself? For Fa? Or for all of them? She didn't know. What she did know was that she was sad and in no hurry to get back to her house. Attempting to control herself, she urged the others to leave. She insisted that she wanted to wheel the harp home by herself.

"We'll put it in the van, Angel, and zip on back," her mother suggested.

"No," Rachel answered quietly. "Today—even if it is just today—I think I should move it myself. Look, I got it here. My idea, so I should be responsible for getting it back."

Ginger smoothed Rachel's hair affectionately. "But we're here. You don't have to do it alone."

Rachel nodded. "I know. But this is important."

Her mother's face looked strained as her patience began to erode. "Enough is enough. You can't get that harp back by yourself."

Then Rachel saw what was happening. As she was trying to avoid involving others in her plans, she was also being unreasonably stubborn and difficult. She kissed her mother on the cheek. "Oh, Mom—let's not argue. I don't want to make trouble. Look, it's less than a mile. If you and Kate go in the van, maybe Sandy'll help me wheel the harp."

"Yes, I will," Sandy said, jumping eagerly into their conversation.

"But, Sandy, your leg," Ginger said. "It's just out of a cast . . ."

"Well, I'm supposed to exercise it as much as possible. So come on, Rachel. Let's go."

That settled that. Ginger and Kate headed for the van while Sandy and Rachel took off with the harp. Rachel had her skates on again, which helped when they went downhill and made things more difficult when they climbed up. But they continued to make progress. Because of the awkward instrument, they were much too busy to hold any coherent conversation. Most of what they had to say were things like:

"Easy on the right."

"Mailbox ahead."

"Light's green now."

"Lady with a baby."

Rachel didn't know how Sandy felt about her at this moment or how he had felt about her Christmas concert, but he seemed glad to be along with her. He didn't call her Wonder Woman, nor did he imply in any way that what she had done had been weird or strange. It would have embarrassed him, she knew, to ask straight out how he felt, so she didn't.

Besides, getting the harp home proved to be a thoroughly exhausting experience. It was neither fun nor exciting, simply very hard work, pushing, steering, negotiating curbs. Sandy didn't complain, but Rachel knew she'd taken on too much for both of them. "Too many ideas," she told herself silently. "Too fast. Too much at once."

It was a long, long struggle. At last, though, the house loomed up before their eyes. Rachel was achy and sweating. Her lovely white dress was damp and dirty. Her hair hung in strings about her face. Her eyes felt swollen. The harp, no doubt, was so badly out of tune by now that it would take her a week to work it back into shape. But they were home.

"Thank you, Sandy," she said, as they wheeled it into

the dining room. "This wasn't one of my better ideas. I think I've still got a long way to go."

Sandy shrugged. "Win some, lose some," he answered, his eyes widening as he caught sight of the African-violet tree with its twinkling white lights. "And don't worry so much, Rachel. You're okay."

Lurching forward wearily, she gave him a little punch in the center of his back. "Thanks," she said.

Then, turning, she dragged herself upstairs to her room. What she needed desperately was another shower. She grabbed for her robe and the damp towel she'd left on the floor that morning. Then, passing Demi, who was asleep on her bed, she staggered out of her room.

She wasn't more than three or four steps down the hall when, belatedly, she realized something. She began to back up. Slowly, ever so slowly, she retraced her steps until she was inside her room again, until she could get a full, clear view of her bed.

There, as she had noticed before, was Demi, asleep. But he was sleeping on something. Something that looked like a little nest. Or pile. A little nest of ribbons. Not very many. Only a few.

Not knowing quite whether to laugh or cry, Rachel shooed Demi away and sat down next to them. Those ribbons were a birthday gift, a Christmas gift. They were the signs of the beginning of a truce. And they'd come from Norm, of that she was certain. His gift in return for hers. He was probably out in the dark hall right now standing close to her mother and peering into her room.

For Rachel there would be no scarlet ribbons piled to the ceiling. Just this small pile. But these ribbons—these precious ribbons—could not possibly have come from anyone except her color-blind stepfather. They were bright, shiny, and green.